Thomas Edgar Pemberton

A Very Old Question

Vol. III

Thomas Edgar Pemberton

A Very Old Question
Vol. III

ISBN/EAN: 9783337044848

Printed in Europe, USA, Canada, Australia, Japan

Cover: Foto ©Andreas Hilbeck / pixelio.de

More available books at **www.hansebooks.com**

A VERY OLD QUESTION.

A Novel.

BY

T. EDGAR PEMBERTON,

AUTHOR OF "UNDER PRESSURE," "DICKENS'S LONDON,"
ETC., ETC.

" For, 'tis a question left us yet to prove,
Whether love lead fortune, or else fortune love."
HAMLET—*Act* iii, *Scene* ii.

IN THREE VOLUMES.
VOL. III.

London:
SAMUEL TINSLEY,
10, SOUTHAMPTON STREET, STRAND.
1877.

CONTENTS OF VOL. III.

A VERY OLD QUESTION.

CHAPTER I.

MINNIE'S MISGIVINGS.

IT is now right that the course of this history should revert to Minnie Tryan, in order that it may be told under what influences she, who was ordinarily so decided in her ideas and actions, had suddenly become so weak and wavering.

It has been seen that owing to unfortunate circumstances, there existed between Minnie and her mother none of that confidence which between mother and daughter one naturally expects to find, and hence it was that Mrs. Tryan was not shown, and knew nothing about, that letter which immediately before his departure for London Hammond had

written. Minnie was accustomed to make
decisions for herself without consulting any-
one, and though at the time she had quite
made up her mind what her answer to the
letter would be, she had no intention of telling
her mother anything about it until between
herself and her lover everything had been
settled.

·And so it came to pass that Mrs. Tryan
was under the impression that, notwithstanding his more than marked attentions to her
daughter, Hammond had taken himself off on
a visit of indefinite length without having
made the " declaration " which not only might
have been expected, but which common justice
surely demanded.

The good lady's indignation and perplexity
may be better imagined than described. If
Minnie had been an ordinary girl with a
" proper pride " of her own, they could have
talked it over together, and probably have
devised some means of bringing the deceiver
to book ; but as we have seen Mrs. Tryan had
sufficient awe of her daughter to make her
altogether silent to her on the subject, and so
she could do nothing but regret her peculiari-

ties, and her own lack of a husband or a son who could boldly have demanded of the fugitive what his intentions were.

For as long as she could she bore it all to herself, but her patience having been further tried by the systematic way in which Minnie silenced her whenever she endeavoured by little hints and questions to bring the conversation round to this interesting point, she one day felt that she could bear it no longer, and so she betook herself to Auracaria Villa, with the avowed purpose of confiding in Kate and of taking her advice on the matter.

To Mrs. Tryan's surprise, however, Kate, instead of giving her the sympathy which she expected, expressed upon the subject most extraordinary views, which to the reader will best be given in her own words.

" Well, mamma," she said, when the whole history had been unfolded to her, " I cannot say that I am surprised to hear this, because it is just what every sensible person must for a long time have foreseen ; indeed it is just what I told Gerald would be sure to happen directly I heard that you were going to take Hammond Rockcliffe into your house. *I* did

not interfere because I have long ago found
out that interference, especially where you
have to deal with such an extraordinary being
as Minnie, is a very thankless task ; but the
way in which he was playing fast and loose
with her, and the way in which she was encouraging him, was so palpable that I certainly
thought that you would see through it, and
put a stop to it before it was too late.   That
Minnie is not capable of taking care of herself
we have known for a very long time, and it is
a very great misfortune, both for herself and
for her relatives, that she has been allowed to
have her own way as much as she has.   The
way in which she disgraced herself by going
to work in a factory will cling to her, and
unluckily through her to us, all her life, and
since Hammond Rockcliffe saw her in that
condition you can hardly feel surprised that
he treated her accordingly.   I suppose that
Minnie took example from her fellow work-
girls, for she certainly encouraged him most
glaringly, and it is no matter of surprise to
me that he tried to take advantage of it.
But what *does* astonish me, mamma, is that
you should have encouraged him too, and that

you should for one moment have thought that
a gentleman of his position, and with his connections, should have entertained honourable
intentions towards Minnie, a little chit who
has done everything in her power to disgrace
us ; a pretty thing indeed it would have been
if *she* should ever have had the chance of
marrying such a man as Hammond Rockcliffe,
and a nice reward for those in the family who
have always striven to maintain its position !
No, mamma, I am a much younger married
woman than you are, but I flatter myself I
can see a little further. In Hammond Rockcliffe's attentions to her, Minnie has simply
reaped the reward of her own foolish doings,
and we may be very thankful that the thing
has stopped where it has. Why, he never
dared to obtrude himself upon me as he has
done upon her, for I always kept my own
position."

In vain did Mrs. Tryan, who was at first
indignant at what she chose to consider Kate's
aspersions, but who afterwards, by reason of
that young lady's determined views on the
point, became conciliatory and nervous ; in
vain did she rake up numberless scenes and

incidents in which Hammond's honourable
intentions had been apparent ; in vain did she
asseverate that a match between him and
Minnie would be by no means out of place ;
in vain did she feebly endeavour to defend
the conduct of her younger daughter. Kate
knew much more upon such subjects than she
did, and so at last the bewildered mother was
almost fain to acknowledge, and she returned
home with a feeling that Hammond Rockcliffe was a most abandoned character, and
that Minnie had had a most lucky escape ;
and just as a mother who has had restored
into her arms a child who has been rescued
from the jaws of accidental death, and who
having gratefully discovered that the de-
livered one is perfectly safe and sound, immediately records her gratitude in the shape
of bodily chastisement as some sort of recom-
pense for her own maternal alarm, and as a
future warning to her offspring,—so did Mrs.
Tryan resolve to deal sternly with Minnie,
and henceforth to keep over her the strictest
watch.

Kate also determined to have with Minnie an
immediate interview on the subject, and with

that intent invited her to come to Auracaria Villa. It is to be feared that Kate's feelings were not wholly unselfish ; of Minnie's discretion and safety she had no fear whatever ; but, though she might perhaps have thought that it would be well to warn her of the dangers of a flirtation with Hammond Rockcliffe, the idea that whereas *she* herself had been content to wed with the son of a Blackhampton mill-owner, her younger and more lightly-estimated sister should have the chance of uniting herself with a member of one of the best county families in the neighbourhood, well nigh drove her mad with jealousy.

What first passed between the sisters need not be told in detail. Kate commenced by telling, with a great assumption of wisdom and experience, pretty much as she had done to her mother, her opinion of Hammond Rockcliffe, and her views concerning his attentions to Minnie. As a matter of course that young lady, being as indignant with Kate for the wrong light in which she saw things as for her unlooked-for interference, was immediately up in arms, and a somewhat sharp encounter of words was the result.

And now it was that Minnie decided that she must no longer keep secret Hammond's letter and proposal. If her intimacy with him had been so marked as to have become notorious, and if that intimacy could be so misconstrued as to induce her sister to speak to her as she had done, she felt that, although until the month had come to an end, and everything was settled, she would gladly have kept the matter to herself, she ought not in common justice to herself, as well as to others, to remain silent any longer.

And so, not without a little mischievous pleasure in the new and unexpected light which she would be able to put upon things, she determined to take Kate into her confidence, and altering her tone, she said :

" I am sure, my dear Kate, that by your warning you mean nothing but kindness, and I ought to feel very much obliged to you for the trouble which you are taking about me and my affairs; but you do not, for one moment, seem to think that it is possible things may be between Mr. Rockcliffe and me just as they once were between yourself and Gerald ?"

"Oh, Minnie, you foolish, foolish girl!" said Kate. "You do not mean, for one moment, to tell me that you think that such a thing is possible?"

"And why not possible?" asked Minnie, saucily, and smiling triumphantly as she thought of her letter.

"Because of Mr. Rockcliffe's family and position. Do you reflect what it is when compared with yours?"

"Oh, that's nonsense," said Minnie, with a laugh; "and as coming from you, it is especially nonsense, Kate. I'm quite sure that you never thought any one was too good for *you;* and notwithstanding my vagaries, you can't get over the fact that I am your sister. I think that the question of family might be got over!"

"Why, you don't mean to tell me," said Kate, "that he has really said anything to you?"

"No, I don't say that he has *said* anything to me," said Minnie.

"Then, Minnie, it is only right that I should speak quite plainly to you, for it is quite evident that you do not know what you are doing, or what you are thinking about. Neither you nor I have ever before had anything to do with a gentleman of Mr. Rockcliffe's position, and it is lucky for you that my knowledge and experience enable me to tell you how lightly such gentlemen are accustomed to estimate any attentions which they choose to bestow on girls in your position, and also what may come to pass if such attentions are allowed to go too far."

"Take care that *you* do not go too far, Kate!" said Minnie, with a heightened colour.

"What I say I say for your good, and because I know that it is my duty," said Kate, calmly; "and if you are foolish enough to be indignant, I cannot help it."

"And what if Hammond Rockcliffe should prove an exception to the rule of your experience, and should ask me to be his wife?"

"Why, I should be very sorry to hear of it."

"And why, Kate? Surely you would not grudge me a good husband?"

"Certainly not; but I should know that if it were possible that Hammond Rockcliffe should become so infatuated as to make you such a proposition, and if you were selfish enough to accept it, there would be nothing but a life of misery in store for both of you."

" And why, pray ?"

" Because your positions are so unequal. Because his relations and friends would have nothing to do with you ; and because, on account of you, they would cut him. Because the time would very soon come when he would only too clearly see how you had managed to drag him down ; because he would then grow tired of you, and tell himself that you had taken advantage of, and had entrapped him !"

" And may I ask, Kate," said Minnie, as quietly as her fast-gathering indignation would allow her, and looking very hard at her sister, " may I ask, Kate, whether, if before you were engaged to Gerald, Hammond Rockcliffe had made you think that he loved you, and would ask you to be his wife, and if you had felt that you loved him, may I ask would all these things then have been so clear to you ?"

" No," said Kate, decidedly ; " because the thing would, to a great extent, have been different. It is true that we are sisters, but

I, I am thankful to say, have always remembered that, though we were poor, we were
born ladies, and so I have never acted as you
have chosen to do. You are sure, Minnie,
sooner or later, to reap the reward of your
obstinacy and folly, while the disgrace of
having worked in that factory will cling to
you as long as you live. Supposing, for the
sake of argument, that such a thing were
possible, and Hammond Rockcliffe had asked
you to become his wife, of course his family
would hear of it, and would want to know
who and what you were. They would only
too soon hear how you had worked in a factory, and therefore naturally they would suppose that he had become infatuated about
some common Blackhampton factory girl !"

"At first they might ; but when they came
to know me——"

" Pooh ! They would never know you ;
they would never have anything to do with
you. Do you think that they would ever
trouble themselves to draw such a fine dis-
tinction as you see in your own mind ? No,
Minnie, if he has ever paid you more than
ordinary attention, you may depend upon it

that it was merely to pass away an idle hour, as men will do with girls who they believe are open to that sort of thing. Whether you have encouraged him or not you know best; but if you have, I do beg that for all our sakes you will at once discontinue anything of the sort."

" I will do what I believe to be best," said Minnie, in a very subdued voice. " Indeed, I have always tried to do that."

" Yes, I do believe that you have," said Kate ; " but you have nevertheless made terrible mistakes, and that is why I now feel bound to talk to and warn you. Goodness knows that I did all that I could to dissuade you from going to Triptree's Mill, and if you had only listened to me then, I should not have had to have spoken to you now. There, let that be an end of it."

And having made her sister thoroughly unhappy, Kate kissed her quite affectionately, and the conversation terminated, for concerning her determination to speak of Hammond's letter, Minnie had suddenly altered her mind.

And indeed her mind had suddenly become full of entirely new thoughts—thoughts which troubled and perplexed her for many and many a day. Until this conversation with Kate, it had never for one moment occurred to her but that her love for Hammond was a thing which, both on his account and her own, it was good to encourage ; and when she had received his letter, she had rejoiced in the thought that she was so ready with her answer, but now she had to consider whether for his sake (and she loved him so well that for him she was prepared to make any sacrifice) she would do right in saying she would become his wife.

In a moment, however, she had put on one side any thought of levity on Hammond's part which Kate's remarks might have suggested. Of his honour she had, of course, on account of her much-prized letter, no doubt ; but, beyond this, there did certainly seem a great deal of common sense in what her sister had said.

Hammond's position was very different to her own ; that there was no gainsaying, and it was not at all likely that his family would look with favour upon his union with her. It was not the first time that this had occurred

to her, but it was the first time that she had
thought that the sentiments of the Rockcliffe
family could be a matter of very great importance to either of them. She was prone to
act for herself, and perhaps, so long as she did
what she believed to be right, to too overmuch
pride herself on caring little for what other
people thought about her; and as she knew
that Hammond owed nothing to his friends,
and to a great extent sympathised with her
in her ideas of independence, she had altogether set the subject on one side. But now
she was regarding it with somewhat different
eyes. Would a marriage with her really,
socially and practically, injure his position and
prospects? Would all his relatives at once
renounce him, and look with contempt on
her? Would they, as Kate had suggested,
think that he had been "entrapped" by a
"factory girl?" for the supposition that they
would hardly be able to distinguish the difference between her avocation at Triptree's Mill
and the life of an ordinary Blackhampton
work-girl certainly seemed reasonable. Would
he in time, and when the troubles of married
life might be pressing heavily upon them,

come to think that he had made a mistake, and regret the irretrievable step which he had taken? Was he not now acting under the influence of an infatuation which she herself had done her utmost to encourage? and, if so, was it not manifestly her duty to prevent future trouble by declining his offer?

Day and night these and many other thoughts perplexed poor Minnie, and with all her might she strove to see clearly her way before her, resolved at any cost to do what might seem to her to be her duty, and best for the welfare of the man whom she loved.

Now she would be influenced by her pride, and anon by her love ; the one would tell her that she had never done anything of which she need be ashamed, that she had worked because she knew it was better to do so, and to earn money upon which to live, than to be supported by charity, and that she was as good as any Rockcliffe that had ever been born ; pride then told her that she ought to think of this, and of herself, and not to place herself in a position to receive the slights of others ; and when pride asserted itself, and she conjured up pictures of the future, in

which she was the victim of aristocratic inso-
lence, and her husband the object of pity for
the mistake which he had made, she told
herself that nothing should induce her to
accept Hammond's offer. And then love
would have its turn, and she would sob her
heart out, telling herself that she must risk
everything, even his happiness, so long as she
married Hammond, the idol of her heart;
and then again love would change its tone,
and she would resolve that if it were once
quite clear to her that it would be better for
him that she should refuse him, that the
strength of her devotion was such as to render
possible any self-sacrifice which might promote
his welfare, or be for his good.

She was in this frame of mind when she
wrote to Hammond, and asked him for more
time.

That married life should not be too hastily
entered into, she had at this time, at Auracaria Villa, a seasonable warning, for notwithstanding Gerald's ardent and unabating
love for Kate, the state of things there was
by no means satisfactory. Gerald, indeed,
loved Kate to a fault, and the consequence of

his never being able to find it in his heart
to deny her anything for which she wished,
was that he not unfrequently provided for
her inevitable and unnecessary trouble. By
nature Kate was petulant and exacting ; she
liked above all things to be waited upon and
to have her every little desire gratified, and
to these traits Gerald, whose great characteristic was his unselfishness, fell an easy
prey. Now, although to have an unselfish
husband, and one who is in every way not
only willing but anxious to sacrifice his inclination and comfort for his wife's, is, as
every lady will allow, a " consummation
devoutly to be wished," it is quite possible
that such a man may, with an exacting wife,
provide for her whom he would most . please,
almost as much trouble as if he had given to
his own selfish propensities a loose rein.

If from the first Gerald had told Kate
what he could afford to provide for her and
what he could not, it is more than possible
that she would have been quite content,
although she might at times have indulged
in vain longings, to have lived happily as
they were; but he was so anxious to please

her, so desirous of proving to her the depth
of his love, that she had only to name a wish,
for him with heart and soul to try and provide it for her, and as his father's name was
well known in Blackhampton, " heart and
soul " meant, at first, not much more than
obtaining things on credit; and he, being of
an anxious temperament, would often lie
awake at night, happy, perhaps, in the
thought that he had, during the day, gratified
a sudden fancy of his now sleeping wife, but
wondering how that, and his other liabilities,
were to be met, and what she would ask for
next. To do her justice, she was quite unconscious of any misgivings on his part of
this sort ; she believed that the wealth of
Mr. Triptree, senior, was enormous, and saw
no reason why Gerald, his eldest son, should
not enjoy a share of it, and her nature was
not one of those which would prompt her to
go without anything for the sake of asking
for it; had he been strong-minded enough
candidly to have told her that he could not
afford for her such and such things, it is to be
imagined that she, being in the main a sensitive, warm-hearted girl, would, notwith-

standing disappointment, have made herself
content ; as it was she was made continually
unhappy by reason of half-realised desires.

For example, the pony carriage, which pre-
vious to their marriage, and in a rash moment,
Gerald had promised to Kate, was a thing
which he knew very well they ought not, at
the outset, to attempt to afford ; but so continually did she remind him of it, that, not
having the courage to disappoint her, he one
day brought home a pretty little pony and a
dainty carriage, supplemented by a small boy
in gorgeous livery. In Kate's pride and
delight in this possession he had temporary
satisfaction and pleasure, which, however,
were destined to be short-lived, for about a
fortnight after its acquisition, and when they
were one afternoon triumphantly driving in
it, they met Mr. Triptree, senior.

"And who the deuce may this turn-out
belong to ?" said he, his voice betraying that
he was in one of the bad humours, which
lately with him had become very common.

Gerald, looking shamefaced, and feeling
guilty, for he had not dared to tell his parent
of the purchase, said nothing, but Kate, who

had no notion of being lightly spoken to by her vulgar father-in-law, answered pertly :

" It belongs to us, of course. Do you think I should care to drive about in a borrowed carriage ?"

" Belongs to you !" cried Mr. Triptree. " And may I ask who has paid, or who is going to pay for it ?"

" I—I—the fact is, sir, I have a source," stammered Gerald, " a source from which I hope shortly to make a great deal of money, and so I promised Kate this little present, and so I have bought it."

" And so I'll trouble you to sell it," said Mr. Triptree, very angrily, and not without some strong language which is here suppressed. " You and your sources ! I know a source which will bring *me* to the workhouse if it isn't checked with a pretty strong hand."

" I think we had better drive on, Gerald," said Kate, with a very stately air. . " At the present time your father evidently does not know how to speak before a lady."

" Drive on ! You'll drive on when I choose, you impudent young hussy !" said the irate Mr.

Triptree, seizing the restive pony by the bridle, and shaking its head roughly; "you'll have to learn how to speak to *me*, and the sooner you do it the better. A pretty one you are to call yourself a 'lady,' and to try to teach me manners! You, who but for my pocket would hardly have a rag to your back!"

"Father!" remonstrated Gerald, "You must not say such things as that; you would not if you were speaking coolly."

"And you hold your tongue, you young fool," replied his father; "you may allow yourself to be gammoned by that young vixen of a wife of yours as much as you choose, and I wish you joy of the precious bargain you've made, but you'll please either to remember what you owe to me, or take the consequences. Now, look here, you'll send back that pony and trap before you go to bed to-night, and then send me word that you've done so, or not another shilling of my money finds its way into your house. Now, mark what I say, for, by the Lord, I mean it!" and releasing the pony's head he strode off.

During their drive home the young couple were silent, for they did not wish that the small boy, who was seated behind them, and who had been the interested and delighted hearer of all that had taken place, should be the witness of anything further, for each felt that there were unpleasant things yet to follow; but arrived at Auracaria Villa, Kate at once commenced an altercation.

"Well!" said she, "I should think that few husbands ever have such an opportunity of sitting by and of hearing their wives insulted as you have had this afternoon. If I had thought, Gerald, that for one moment you would have given way in this business to your father, I would——"

"My dear wife," interrupted the unhappy Gerald, "don't say anything more, because I am afraid that I must——"

"Must what?" demanded she.

"Give way, Kate. You see, being unluckily to a certain extent dependent on my father, I am bound to defer to his wishes."

"You are bound to do nothing of the sort, and if you go on in this spiritless way we shall soon have no wills of our own. You must now, once and for all, Gerald, make a stand against your father's tyranny and bearishness."

" I am afraid, Kate," answered Gerald, with a feeble attempt at a smile, " that we should not be able to stand out long ; we are not provisioned for a siege."

" Pooh !" said Kate, " what a coward you are ; you seem to have no idea of getting your own way, but give in at once. I believe if your father told you you must go and stand for a whole day on your head in the middle of the road you would give a meek sigh and then, without a word, go out and try to do it ! If you had spoken to him this afternoon as one man ought to have spoken to another, if you had shown him plainly that you resented his interference, and declined to sit by while your wife was insulted, he would have given way in a moment."

" I told him that he ought not to have spoken to you as he did, and I am very sorry, Kate, that he so far forgot himself; but from some cause or other he has lately become very testy, and often says things which he does not mean. If you think an apology necessary, I must make it on his behalf; but with regard to resenting his interference, I must tell you frankly, dear wife, that, while everything which we have in the world belongs in reality to him, and while we are dependent upon him for our subsistence, I do not see how I can help it."

"Then do you mean to say," cried Kate, with flashing eyes, " that you are going to submit to him, and that you will sell my pony ?"

" Dear, dear Kate," said Gerald, "if in this I give way to my father, it is only because I know it will be for our ultimate good. Directly I myself can afford it, and I will work with my whole strength by day and by night to do it, I will get another pony for you, and give it to you as gladly as I would anything in the world for which you asked."

" No you would not !" returned his wife. "I begin to see it now. You married me on false promises, and now that you know I cannot go back, you are going to trample on me, and you are in league with your wretched, vulgar, purse-proud, miserly father, against me !"

" Kate !" said Gerald, now in his turn

angry also, "you do not think what you are saying. I have never yet spoken severely to you, but you *shall* not in my presence say such things of my kind and generous father. Here, in a house which his bounty has provided for us, standing among furniture which he has given us, literally living upon him, it is unseemly to a degree. Pray understand me when I say that I *will* not allow you to do it, and that I recognise his right to have a voice in the amount of our expenditure."

It was the first time that Gerald had spoken harshly to his wife, or had endeavoured to lay down the law to her, and it may confidently be assumed that it was also the last, for to his dying day he carried with him the remembrance of the scene which followed.

From indignant remonstrances and loud lamentations, Kate relapsed into copious tears, and from tears into violent hysterics. Now, at this time her state of health was such as to make to an anxious husband, who, if he had received one had received a thousand cautions on no account to excite his wife, such a state of mind, peculiarly distressing and alarming, and Gerald, who had quite made up his mind to be firm, gave way in a moment, and cursed himself for having been such a fool as to have forgotten himself.

In vain, however, he implored for pardon, in vain he endeavoured to impart consolation, in vain did he promise her all the horses and carriages in Christendom, provided only she would endeavour to calm herself; for between her sobs and cries Kate could (or would) do nothing but deplore her unhappy lot, regret that she had ever bestowed affection on a husband who ill-used her, and pray that she might be speedily removed from so miserable a world; and Gerald's position was soon rendered worse, inasmuch as the servant-girl, who came to the rescue, and who, in her heart of hearts cordially liked her master, and as cordially hated her mistress, at once grasped the situation, and making the matter one of sex, sided entirely with the latter, and without having heard a single word of what had passed (for she had been in the backyard with a young man from the baker's), wondered how "he could ever have said such things to the poor creature," and so forth, to the end of the established chapter.

It was a long time before anything like a compromise could be made, but finally the luckless pony carriage was sent off for Mrs. Tryan, that she might come and condole with her unhappy daughter, and Gerald sallied forth on a mission to his father's, to endeavour to persuade him to alter his views anent that unfortunate speculation.

The conversation which took place at The Shrubs, and the intelligence which he learned there, were not, however, of a nature to re-assure him, but rather to render him more uneasy than before. Mr. Triptree, whom he found alone, smoking cigars and drinking whisky and water, displayed no passion when he hesitatingly made his request, that he would reconsider his decision with regard to the disposal of the pony-carriage, but he eyed his son gloomily and said not unkindly :

" It would have been better for you, my lad, if I'd never altered my decision about your marrying that girl, but you got me on my good-natured side and I let you have your own way. Well, that's all done with now, and it's no use crying over spilt milk, but I'm afraid, Gerald, you'll have a fearful time of it with her."

" I hope, my dear father, that you do not for one moment think that Kate and I are not on 'all points of one mind ?"

" Of one mind ? Lord bless you, my boy, when you're as old as me, and understand something about women, you'll drop that idea that there ever was a husband and wife of one mind. There's many who has got common sense, and, through making up their minds to it, pull well together, but it's a question. of give and take with every one, and your wife's one of those who'll want to do all the taking and none of the giving."

" Kate is very delicate, father, and very sensitive, and perhaps to strangers she may at times appear to be a little petulant, but to *me*, I assure you, she is always the same."

" Aye, and always will be," said Mr. Trip-tree, with a short laugh. " It's all very well now, perhaps ; you think you'll never be tired of waiting on her hand and foot, and of sacrificing your comfort for hers, but the time will come, my lad, when you'll like to have your slippers fetched for you, and your grog

mixed, and it'll seem hard lines to have to be
up all night because your wife's got a cold in
the head, Depend upon it a wife's a better
and a happier woman when her husband lets
her do something for him instead of his doing
everything for her."

" The danger of that doctrine," said Gerald,
" is that you would be so apt to go too far on
the other side."

" That's pretty safe in the hands of most
women," said Mr. Triptree ; adding with
another short laugh, " I don't think *you* need
feel alarmed on that score."

Seeing that his father was now in a fairly
good humour, Gerald laughed also, and
ventured once more to speak of the pony-
carriage ; immediately it was mentioned, however, Mr. Triptree again became gloomy.

" No, Gerald," said he, "you can't catch
me on my good-natured side on that subject,
and I'll tell you why. I've been deuced hard
hit lately and have lost a pot of money.
Time was when no man could get over me,
but times have changed, and there are such a
d——d lot of rogues and swindlers in the
market, and such a d——d lot of complicated

ways of letting people in, that a man who wants to get more than five per cent. for his money had need to have eyes all round his head. I've only two, and I begin to think that they're not half as sharp as they used to be, for I was let in the other day, and again yesterday, in a way that makes me ashamed to look at my own face in the glass when I'm shaving, and if one or two more things, as is threatening, go wrong, curse me if I shall be able to do so, and so when you see me growing a beard, you'll know the cause of it. I can't afford, Gerald, to allow you a penny more than I do now, and if I'm hit again, I mayn't be able to allow you as much. When I'm actually selling off some of my own nags it's hardly the time to ask me to give you a pony and trap."

" You don't really mean, father, that your losses are so heavy that you are obliged to sell any of the horses ?"

" But I do mean it, sir. Yesterday, for the first time for thirty years, I didn't know where to look for money. I'd a big bill to meet, and my credit to keep up, and ' Brown Stout ' had to find some of the coin. That's why you met me walking home."

"Oh, father, I am so sorry; I know what store you set by that horse."

" Perhaps now, then, you'll understand why I was a bit riled when I met you swelling about in a turn-out which I knew I should be expected to pay for, and then to be sauced by that impudent chit of a wife of yours. I didn't mean to tell you all this, Gerald, for I'm one of those who think it best to keep their affairs to themselves, but after moping here by myself it seems a comfort to talk a bit."

" I am very glad that you have told me, father, for I can assure you that it will influence my actions very much. Oh, father, if I could ever do anything to help you—anything to prove to you my gratitude for all you have done for me."

Gerald took his father's hand in his. Mr. Triptree shook it kindly, and then, taking a copious draught from his tumbler, pushed the spirit-bottle to Gerald, who, however, declined to take it.

" You're right, you're right," said the father; " keep independent of it as long as you can. When I was a young man, and first began to make my way, I had many a hard and anxious day's work, and I always made it a rule never to touch stimulants till the work was done. When I'd made my way, and could afford to enjoy myself, I was freer with the bottle. Now that I've again got anxious things about me, and anxious work to do, I find I can't tackle it till I've pretty well soaked myself with spirits, and that worries me so that I keep on drinking more to forget it. When a man begins to depend on the bottle, Gerald, he loses confidence in himself, and becomes no good."

" But you can't call yourself a slave to the bottle, father," said Gerald, in a tone of remonstrance.

Mr. Triptree made no reply, but mixed himself another glass. ·

Before he took his leave, Gerald, remembering what awaited him at Auracaria Villa, put in one more plea on behalf of Kate.

" Father," he said, " you know that just at the present time it is important that Kate should be neither vexed nor excited. Do you think I might manage to keep the pony for her until she is well and strong again ?"

"No," said Mr. Triptree; "you will soon have extra expense in another way, and that's the very reason why you ought to get rid of this one. You shall bring the whole concern to me to-morrow morning, and I'll sell it for you."

As Gerald walked home, he hardly knew whether to be most unhappy about the house which he was leaving, or about the one to which he was going. He was unselfishly sorry to hear of his father's losses, and was grieved to think that he should have to part with the horses which he loved; and to him personally these losses were a most serious matter, all the more so because it was manifest that his father doubted his own power of coping with his difficulties, and sought in the whisky-bottle for the strength which he found wanting in himself. This being the case, where would his losses end? For some time past Mr. Triptree's tendency to self-indulgence had been noticeable, but in his son's eyes, at least it had been venial, for surely he who had worked so hard, and had at one period of his life lived so frugally, had a right now to enjoy himself as he thought fit; but now that stimulants were resorted to as a solace and an assistance, the habit assumed a more serious complexion.

Of course, after what he had just heard, it was apparent to him that instead of adding to his expenses, as it was Kate's daily desire, and, for her sake, his constant inclination to do, it was his duty to his father, his wife, and the child he expected so soon to be born to him, to live as economically as possible ; and this was so manifest to him that he told himself that all trifling must be at an end, and, let the result be what it would, Kate must realise their position, and take the best which he could give her. The poor fellow did not for one moment think that it was her duty too to deny herself and to help him in his honourable aims, or what a happiness to him it would be if only she would show herself willing to do so; but, on the contrary, he harassed and tortured himself with vain longings that he might be able to provide her with her every wish, and pitied her more than himself for the disappointment which, when she came to hear of the failure of his errand, she would undergo.

And yet he might assuredly have bestowed upon himself some little pity for the scene which that night took place at Auracaria Villa. When he reached home he found Mrs. Tryan in possession, and, rousing herself for the occasion, that admirable mother defended her daughter, and spoke her mind out to admiration. Having firmly made up his mind that he must do so, he told them plainly that the pony must go, and that, in consequence of his father's losses, their expenses would probably have to be curtailed, and then, having decided that his behaviour should be a sort of compromise between that of the oak and the reed of Æsop, prepared himself for the storm.

And a very pretty storm it was, notwithstanding the fact that its source might have well been contained in the proverbial tea-cup. Having told her daughter, with many terms of endearment, that it behoved her to be calm— having arranged her on the sofa, and observed that the strictest quiet was absolutely necessary for her, Mrs. Tryan at once proceeded to raise in her presence as great a tempest of words as could possibly have jarred upon the nerves

of a supposed invalid. Commencing by abus-
ing Mr. Triptree—which, separately and col-
lectively, for his conduct to herself, for his
insulting behaviour to Kate, and for his parsi-
mony to his son, she did—she descended with
all her force upon Gerald, and for his submis-
sion to his father, and for his inconsiderateness
to his wife in her present critical condition,
rated him soundly; but he, though he winced
under the lash of her tongue, and could almost
have joined Kate in her continual sobs, sym-
pathising with her as he did with his whole
heart, knew that he must stand his ground,
and, though his words were all conciliatory,
could not be induced to waver one iota in his
determination to defer to the wishes of his
father.

At one period of her oration Mrs. Tryan
expressed her determination at once to re-
move her daughter from the house of Mr.
Triptree's providing, and which, she declared,
had "struck a chill through her" the very
first time she had entered it ; but finding
that even this threat failed to move Gerald,
she decided to sacrifice herself by remaining
in it until further notice, for after what

had taken place she would, she declared, on
no account lose sight of Kate for a single
moment.

This arrangement necessitated the giving
up by Gerald of his share of his wife's room
to his mother-in-law, but this he minded the
less inasmuch as it would enable him to devote some of the hours of the night to that
which was now his one hope and consolation ;
and so, when the storm had subsided, and the
ladies had retired, he betook himself to his
little workshop, and laboured hard at his
darling pump.

Oh, what ardent hopes he built upon the
success of this apparatus !   In it he saw the
solution of all their troubles.   With the fortune which by it he would make, he would
repay his father's losses, he would surround
Kate with every available luxury, and he
would secure for himself name and fame.
And of its success he never for one moment
doubted : he had so nursed and cherished his
project that where practical outsiders would
have seen damning objections, he could only
see natural difficulties which, by reason of the
ingenuity with which they would be over-

come, would form some of the chief advantages of his invention. He had it all " on
paper, as clear as noonday," but he did not
mean to introduce his machine to the public
until it was " absolutely perfect."

And so he patiently toiled on upon an
instrument which, although exquisitely ingenious in many of its details, would to the
uninitiated have appeared about as practically
useful for a pump as for a policeman.

Whether the infant Triptree who a few
weeks later was born into the world was, as
Mrs. Tryan unhesitatingly declared, hastened
on to the commencement of his career on
account of the pony carriage incident, it is
difficult to say, but certainly the poor little
fellow was sufficiently diminutive and weakly
to warrant her assertion : and as this arrival
necessitated the institution of a nurse, and
also the prolongation of Mrs. Tryan's visit,
the sanguine inventor, though he had more
time at his own disposal, became more than
ever apprehensive as to the condition of his
monetary resources.

In these days Auracaria Villa was not a
pleasant house to live in, and but for Minnie,

who came and went frequently, it is probable that its master would have been altogether neglected, and compelled to seek his meals abroad.

But short as Minnie's visits were she always seemed to leave upon the place a brightening effect, and when she was in the house Kate was less peevish, the nurse more inclined to sobriety, Mrs. Tryan less officious and domineering, and even the baby Triptree roared less lustily than was his wont.

But when the time came when the young mother was strong again, when Mrs. Tryan had returned home, when the nurse was drinking at the expense of another householder, and when the baby Triptree was beginning to renounce his lobster-like hue in favour of the normal colour of his species, then the state of discomfort grew from bad to worse, and except to Gerald, who still loved his wife as tenderly as ever he had done, Auracaria Villa became miserable to a degree.

For Kate, finding that her desires for luxury could in no way be gratified, and suffering bitterly under the disappointment (for had she not been led to believe that once married all the pinching and contriving which she hated so bitterly would be at an end ?) lost all interest in her home, in her personal appearance, and ostensibly in her very existence ; and instead of looking the slight, trim, elegant girl who had attracted the notice of everyone, was slovenly in her attire and dejected in her demeanour.

And now it was that Minnie began to comprehend the miseries of ill-assorted and too hasty marriages, and hence was continually torturing herself with the picture of Hammond neglectful of his home, and tired of the wife whom his own family would not acknowledge. And indeed, though she entertained a strong natural affection for her mother and sister, she could not, differing from them though she did, but ask herself, was she fit to become the wife of such a man ? setting on one side the question of her having stooped to manual labour in a manufactory, were her relatives such as with whom he ought to be connected ?

And while these doubts were perplexing her, there came to her, in the shape of another lover, yet another hint. This was no less a

personage than that Mr. Albert Groutage,
who has, in the pages of this history, already
appeared as the manager of the room in Triptree's mill, in which Minnie had worked.   Of
Mr. Groutage little has already been said, but
enough probably to show that, at any rate, in
his own estimation, he was an individual of
no small importance.   His parents were work-
people, good, honest folks, but of the lower
and uneducated type ; and the son had by
praiseworthy ambition, industry, and perseverance secured for himself a very excellent
education, made himself a complete master of
the trade which he followed, and in many
ways put himself very far in advance of the
ordinary run of his fellow-workmen.   The
result of this was that he was so idolised by
his relatives and friends that he began to think
a very great deal too much of himself.   Albert
Groutage, the humble and self-educated work-
man, and the master of his craft, endeavouring
to do good among his less endowed work-
fellows was admirable in the extreme ; but
Albert Groutage, the self-conceited and in-
flated egotist, caring, so long as he himself
was prominently before them, little or nothing

for his inferiors or superiors was objectionable to a degree.

It was for public life that Mr. Albert Groutage felt that his peculiar qualifications were best adapted, and to shine in public life was his soul's ambition. That such a man, in such a town as Blackhampton, should have, as a fit and proper representative of the working-classes, a large body of admirers and supporters was a matter of course, and his frothy oratory, and machine-like elocution, were alike largely admired. On all subjects Mr. Groutage was equally at home ; not only was he able to inform the Ministry how in perplexing situations the country might best be managed and governed, but he could show (in theory) how a working man, earning eighteen shillings a week, and having therewith to support a wife and eight children, could, by becoming a Good Templar, and eschewing tobacco, become a man of affluence.

It would perhaps be wrong to say that the real working men gave him much real support ; his admirers were chiefly young men of similar tastes and ambitions as his own, and to whom

to deliver themselves of blatant orations at
any public meeting which would tolerate
them, was their great idea of earthly happiness, and among these he was preeminent.
Many rebuffs this young aspirant had received,
but he was blessed with what is sometimes
called a remarkably " thick skin ;" and had at
length, by dint of an undeviating course of
persistent obtrusiveness and officiousness,
gained for himself a sufficiently well-known
name as to render him inordinately conceited
and self-sufficient.

That a gentleman so preoccupied should
have little thought or time to bestow on the
frivolous engagement of love-making was a
matter of course, and indeed it was among his
fellow-workpeople a notorious fact that Mr.
Albert Groutage had never been known to
" walk out " or to " keep company " with any-
one ; but it was none the less a fact that this
rising star, being but human, did occasionally
bestow a passing thought to the fascinations
of the fairer sex, and that not least among the
things concerning which he delighted to plume
himself, was the indisputable fact that when
the time came when he should choose to select

for himself a wife, a whole bevy of admiring damsels awaited his beck and call.

The natural result of this was that Mr. Groutage felt that he could well afford to be particular, and it was not for a long time after he had commenced to cast about his critical eye that it alighted with favour upon Minnie Tryan. He was a sufficiently good judge to see that Minnie was, among the girls with whom he most naturally asso- ciated, one by herself, and admiring her for her courage in casting off the prejudices of class, and for coming to work because she knew that work was necessary for her liveli- hood ; appreciating her because her superior education and pleasant, lady-like manners shone among those by whom in the workshop she was surrounded, to the greatest possible advantage, and being, furthermore, by no means unsusceptible to her personal charms, he was no very long time in coming to the conclusion that Minnie was his "destiny," and that just as he had been ordained to emancipate his fellow-men (from what he hardly knew), and to exalt himself (in any way which was the easiest), so he felt that

she had been created to become the humble
sharer in his ambitious work, the helpmate of
his hours of toil, and the solace of his leisure
moments.

It was not Mr. Groutage's intention to
devote much of his valuable time to courtship.
Having made his choice he had no idea but
that it would follow "as the night the day"
that he would be gratefully accepted; but
being also most anxious that in such an
important step he should make no mistake,
he, before speaking to Minnie of his decision,
called on Mrs. Tryan, and informed her that
it was, with the view of becoming better
acquainted with her daughter, and of judging
of her qualifications for becoming his wife, his
desire to be allowed to visit at her home.

Without feeling strongly disposed towards
this suitor, but believing that his existence
might act as a timely spur to the recreant
Hammond, Mrs. Tryan gave him the desired
permission, and Mr. Groutage became regular
in his visits; and although from the very first
Minnie, who at once divined their object,
endeavoured to make as plain as possible her
views upon the subject, they not only con-

tinued, but it became in Blackhampton gene-
rally known in what quarter Mr. Groutage
was "paying his attentions."

And now the reader will understand who
the Blackhampton gentleman, with whose existence Mrs. Tryan had endeavoured to make
Hammond Rockcliffe uncomfortable, was.

Minnie's feelings upon the matter were very
consistent. Not only did she from the very
moment when she first suspected Mr. Groutage's intentions towards her make up her
mind what her answer should be, but so
annoyed was she at his proceedings that she
even looked forward to the time when he
might condescend to acquaint her with their
purport, and ask her to become his wife, that
she might have the malicious pleasure of
noting his astonishment when for his answer
he would receive a direct and decided "No."
But in the meantime the poor girl learnt, or
thought she ought to learn, another bitter
lesson; for if a man like this believed that in
asking her to marry him, he paid her a compliment, and if her own mother, by allowing
his visits, acknowledged that such a thing
would be not unsuitable but acceptable, how

wrong would it on her part be to dream of
becoming the wife of such a man as Hammond
Rockcliffe !

This was how matters stood on that Sunday
when Hammond came down from London
and found her in such a state of indecision.

And very shortly after this, fuel was added
to the fire which was burning in her poor
breast, by " young Fred," the son of Anthony
Northover, who having returned from a brief
visit to London, and meeting Minnie at Auracaria Villa, referred to having called upon his
cousin in Wimpole Street, and gave a vivid
account of that establishment.

" My eye," said this engaging youth, " no-
body who wasn't used to London life and
London ways would credit the way things are
going on there ! Hammond Rockcliffe, the
young doctor who was down here, makes use
of the house just as though it were his own,
and, blow me, if an outsider wouldn't say that
he was the husband and Percy the visitor.   I
dessay I was down on it more than most
would have been, for I remember old times,
when both of them were after her, and it was
a toss-up which would marry her.   Why

Percy's such a fool as to let things go on as they're going on now, I don't know. Hammond's there morning, noon, and night; lunches there, dines there, and takes her to the theatre and what not; and I can assure you that at the West End it's getting a regular growing scandal! Of course, as Gertrude's my cousin, I felt in a delicate position, or else once or twice I really felt as though I must interfere; but Percy's such an easy, good-natured, go-ahead sort of fellow, that I hadn't the heart to say anything to him, and sooner than drag myself into it, I made up my mind to let the thing drift; but mark my words, if you keep your eyes upon the papers, you'll see what'll come of the goings-on *there!*"

And then it was that Minnie, knowing what she did of Hammond's old associations with Gertrude, felt that the land upon which she had fondly thought to be so happy, was going from beneath her feet, and that by her all hope of becoming his wife must be given up.

CHAPTER II.

GERALD'S INGENUITY.

PATIENTLY and laboriously working at his complicated pump, and becoming now and again, and in spite of himself, bewildered, if not disheartened, at the difficulties which intervened between it and perfection, Gerald was one day suddenly seized with inspiration. Somewhat after the fashion of the mountain in labour which brought forth a mouse, so his intricate machinery suddenly presented to him an idea for a novel corkscrew! At the first blush he was inclined to put the thing on one side as puerile, and even to be irritated that anything so trivial should, while he was engaged on so important a work, occur to him; but the thing seemed to him so good in itself, that he was soon fascinated by it, and he told himself that great inventors can afford to dabble alike in small as well as large things ; that Watt himself, before he perfected the steam-engine, had spent some of his time over the modest but useful copying-press ; and that numerous other great inventors had bequeathed to posterity numberless anecdotes of a similar nature, which to the inquiring aspirant are always ready at hand to be taken as a tonic.

Without, therefore, setting on one side his more ambitious project, he hailed with delight his newly-born corkscrew, and congratulated himself at having, at so critical a time in his career, hit upon something which, though it might not make his fortune, would assuredly bring in for him a very welcome supply of ready money.

It was not long before he found a name for his invention. It was while he was meditating on the simplicity and advantages of the time-honoured, if primitive, screw of Archimedes, that the idea had suggested itself to him ; and he dreamt the next night of the time when " Triptree's Patent Archimedian Self-Acting Corkscrew," would become one of

39—2

the necessities of every English cork-drawing household.

Having made, as far as lay within his power, a perfect model of this ingenious instrument, he decided that not an hour must be lost in securing it by a patent; and indeed, from the moment when the idea had first struck him, to that when he had it ready, he suffered a torment of anxiety lest the same thing should be brought out by any one else, while in every man whom he met he imagined that he saw one who would assuredly forestall him. To say that all inventors are suspicious, would be unfair and untrue, but to say that most of them are, is a matter of fact. Gerald was in this respect one of the many, and dreading lest his precious discovery should be pirated, resolved at any cost to go to the very best patent agent in Blackhampton—a man whom he was convinced would take no advantage of him.

With palpitating heart, therefore, he sought audience of this authority, and with nervous and trembling hands untied his parcel and laid upon the table the first-born of " Triptree's Patent Archimedian, Self-Acting Corkscrews."

"H'm," said the agent, after a long pause, during which he had narrowly eyed the article in question, and, as Gerald thought, superciliously; "h'm—now what do you want me to do for you ? Do you want to instruct or to consult me ?"

"Well, both," said Gerald, surprised at the question; "I want you to take out a patent for me, but certainly I should be glad also to have your opinion."

"H'm," said the agent again. "Are you aware whether this same thing has ever been invented and brought out before ?"

"Good Heavens, no !" cried Gerald, turning pale at the horrible supposition. "You do not mean to tell me that it has !"

"Certainly not," said the agent, smiling; "but it is possible. Corkscrews are articles which have exercised the ingenuity of many inventors, and your first step should be to have a search made."

"I don't think that that would be necessary," said Gerald. "When you asked me the question you frightened me, for I thought for the moment that you knew some one else who had brought it out ; but, if you come to

think of it, it is impossible, for every one
would have heard of it."

"Not as a matter of course," said the
agent. "Many inventors take out patents
which are never worked."

"But even supposing that," said Gerald,
"I conclude I should soon discover my misfortune by having my application for a patent
refused ?"

"Not at all," was the reply. "You can
take out a patent for anything, but when you
have paid your fees you may find yourself
wholly unable to protect it. You, the inventor, are supposed to know what you are
doing, and it is left to you to find out whether
you are first in the field."

"Then you mean to say that two men can
take out patents for the same thing? That
is a horrible defect in the law."

"Possibly; but, being the case, it shows
you how careful you ought to be—that is to
say, if money is any object to you. In my
office, however, I never, unless thoroughly
convinced that an invention is an absolute
novelty, allow a patent to be taken out until
a thorough search has been made."

" Then I suppose it must be done. Will it cost much ?"

" Of course it cannot be done without expense. Shall you be offended, Mr. Triptree, if I ask you a plain question ?"

" Certainly not."

" Would the cost of taking out a patent be a consideration to you ?"

" Indeed, sir, it would. Unless I was convinced that I should make a profit by it, I should be by no means justified in incurring it."

" Then, my dear Mr. Triptree, pardon me if, as an old man, experienced in inventions and in patents, I speak frankly to you, a young and sanguine man. Your invention is exceedingly ingenious, in many respects it is admirable, but, except as a pretty toy, it is valueless."

" On what grounds, sir ?" asked Gerald, almost speechless with astonishment.

" I am sorry to crush your hopes, but it is for your good that I speak plainly. Consider for a moment. Does it supply a want ? There are many corkscrews already before the public ; are not any or all of these good enough for all intents and purposes? But even supposing that your invention is superior to anything among them, I see in it, in its present form, and I don't see that you can alter it, a fatal objection."

" And that is?" asked Gerald ruefully.

" The cost at which they would come. There is in this a great deal of elaborate workmanship, and I am convinced that they could not be produced to sell at less than half-a-guinea a piece."

" And do you think, sir, that for a really good article the public think so much of price?"

" When they can get an article which answers the purpose equally well, at about one tenth the price, I think that they do. I do not say that your corkscrew has not its advantages ; it has many, but not sufficient to command so high a price."

" Then you decline to patent it ?"

" Certainly not," said the agent again smiling. " If you instruct me, I shall of course be happy to do the business for you, and, indeed, it is to do business that I am here ; but I do not like to see a man, who frankly tells me that he cannot well afford to lose money, lay out a considerable sum which I do not think he is likely to see or hear of again."

" But with regard to my corkscrew, of course you may be quite wrong ?"

" Granted.—I may. But I have had much experience in such matters, and I am convinced that I am right. I trust that I have not offended you ?"

" Oh no ? Naturally I am a good deal disheartened and disappointed, but, knowing that if you consulted your own advantage, you would have given me just a contrary opinion, I can only thank you. I can't yet think quite as you do about it, but I think the best plan will be for me to take it home and think it over and see you again in a few days."

"Yes : that will be the best, and I feel quite sure that you will soon think as I do. Take courage Mr. Triptree ! That you have plenty of ingenuity there is no doubt, and in a short time you will probably bring out something about which I, and everyone else, will say :—'here is a good thing,'—take out your patent at once "

But though Gerald could not but feel that

this honestly given opinion was one which
ought greatly to influence him, he could not
yet reconcile himself to the idea that his precious corkscrew was a failure ; after all, he
argued to himself, this was the opinion of
one man only, and though it had been given
in a most straightforward manner, it was unde-
niably that of one of the old school, who could
hardly grasp the requirements of modern days,
and who could still less understand modern
extravagance, which taught people to regard
half-a-guinea in about the same ratio as that
in which our forefathers looked upon a sixpence.

Thus thinking he determined to take another
opinion, and this time he selected the office
of a recently-established patent agency, which
was much given to advertisement and which
was no doubt of the pushing go-ahead sort.

In this firm there were two partners, and
in their united presence Gerald soon found
himself, while the " Self-acting Archimedian
Corkscrew " once more underwent the ordeal
of critical examination.

" Well, sir," said one of the partners, after
each had examined it, and between them a

nod of manifest approval had been exchanged ;
" it is, I can assure you, a pleasure when,
among the bushels of chaff which find their
way into a patent agent's office, a grain of
good corn occasionally comes to the surface.
You are certainly to be congratulated. This
is about the cleverest thing I have seen for a
long time."

" And, moreover, it's just what's wanted,"
said the other partner.

" Oh, you think it does supply a want ?"
said Gerald, who, though intensely delighted,
was resolved that he would move with the
greatest possible caution.

" My dear sir ! Did you ever undergo the
ordeal of seeing one of your maid servants,
or, worse still, your wife, uncork a bottle ?
Why, I consider that the old-fashioned corkscrew spoils more wine than anything else, for
no woman seems able to use it without agita-
ting the bottle as though it contained a
doctor's mixture with directions, ' to be well
shaken before taken.' "

" I believe there are one or two patents
already before the public ?" said the other
partner.

"Yes,—and a precious lot they are. I've bought 'em all, one after the other, and they all lie in the dust-bin. I took home the latest a week ago; gave it the servant to see what she would make of it; she tried it on a bottle of sherry; neck of bottle broke off short in her hand; wine—a nice dry Amontillado, wasted, and worse than that, poor girl's hand badly cut, and so full of bits of broken glass, that we had to send her to the hospital; good useful girl, and my wife in a devil of a mess without her, I can tell you. That's the *last* patent!"

"I consider," said Gerald, "that one of its greatest advantages is that you can uncork a bottle without in the least degree disturbing its contents. My only fear is that the thing would cost too much."

"Cost! What, my dear sir, is the outlay of a few shillings compared with the fact, that for the whole term of your life you would get your wine decently decanted? Look how it would pay a big firm of wine merchants to take this thing up and send out a screw with every case of six dozen ordered! You'd find a hundred ready to jump at the idea;

only of course it'll pay you best to introduce it to the public."

"I shouldn't mind selling it for a good round sum," said the happy Gerald.

" Shouldn't you, by Jove, then——"

" Come, come," said the more silent partner, interrupting this loquacious gentleman ; "all this is premature, though I think you have heard sufficient, Mr Triptree, to see what we think of your invention. For the purpose for which it is intended, we believe it to be admirably adapted ; we believe that it supplies a want, and consequently, the demand for it would be great, and its success, therefore, considerable."

" I need hardly say," said Gerald, " that I am very glad to hear you say so. My only fear was of the cost, and that would not have occurred to me had not Mr.——" (here he mentioned the name of the patent agent to whom he had first been), "suggested it to me."

At this juncture, both the partners looked grave, and the talkative one, who had been again examining the corkscrew, with apparent delight, drawing with it legions of fictitious corks, laid it solemnly upon the table.

"We were not aware, Mr. Triptree," said the other partner, "that we were dealing with a matter which had already been taken to another office. Pardon us if we say that before you allowed us to speak so openly to you, you should have apprised us of this fact."

"If I have committed any breach of etiquette," said Gerald, "I can assure you that I am sincerely sorry, and that I never meant to do so. It simply arose in this way : I took my invention to Mr. ——, and he, while acknowledging its ingenuity, gave it as his opinion that its cost would ruin its chances of success."

"And so it would," said the loquacious partner, "if the world were made up of such men as he, who looks an hour at a fourpenny-bit before he can make up his mind to change it. How could he, I should like to know, who wouldn't know whether wine as thick as mud were not in as good condition as wine as clear as crystal, give an opinion worth two-pence on an invention like this ?"

"That is beside the question," said the other. "The thing is this : If Mr. Triptree has already negotiated with Mr. —— for securing his invention, he ought not to have brought it to us, for it is not likely that we can take work out of another office. On the other hand, I may tell Mr. Triptree, for his information, that patent agents have their specialities, and that in taking this to Mr. —— he took it to the wrong place, and one in which he was as unlikely to get good advice as though he went to consult a lawyer about his health, or a surgeon upon a point of law. All this, Mr. Triptree, I say with the greatest possible respect for Mr. ——, who in his peculiar line of business stands A 1."

"All of which," cried Gerald, " I began to see from the moment when I came here. I am not in any way bound to Mr. ——, and shall only be too glad if you will take the thing in hand for me."

" Upon your assurance that you are not bound to Mr. —— we shall be glad to do so. I take a note, then, that you instruct us to proceed ?"

" There are one or two questions," said Gerald, growing rather bewildered and feeling somewhat awe-stricken at the sight of the ominous-looking printed forms which were now produced, " which I should like to ask. Is it necessary that a search should be made to ascertain whether anything of a similar construction has been patented before ?"

" We always institute a search."

" Will that be costly ?"

" We shall make you our regular charges ; of these no one has ever yet complained."

" Nor am I likely to do so. Now I am very ignorant in these matters, and should be grateful for your advice. Having obtained my patent, what should be my next step ? I said a few moments ago that I should not object to sell it for a good sum, and I thought, sir, that you seemed almost inclined——"

" So I was—so I should be," said the talkative partner, to whom Gerald was now speaking ; " but the fact of your having taken it to Mr. —— renders it out of the question, for which I'm truly sorry."

" Indeed, sir, I think you think too much of that circumstance. I'm sure if I saw Mr. —— and explained the matter to him——"

" Don't do such a thing on any account.

No, sir, the etiquette of the profession renders
it impossible for me to have anything to do
with it. Your best plan will be to get a
manufacturer to take it up—you'll find no
difficulty ; a good thing like that doesn't go
about begging, I can tell you. We'll give
you a list of the most likely people."

And after a little more conversation, after
signing some papers, after handing over some
money and making an early engagement to
hand over some more, Gerald, amid the
congratulations of the partners, took his
leave.

It was not without much difficulty—indeed,
it was not without borrowing from his friends
(a practice to which he resorted for the first
time), that he raised the money to pay the
fees, duties, and charges for his patent ; but
he was now sanguine of success, and for him
it was a proud day when he conveyed to
Auracaria Villa a portentous document, attached to about a couple of pounds of bees-
wax, encased in a tin box, and bearing the
impression of the Great Seal of England.

His next step was to try his luck with the
manufacturers, and from the list with which

the patent agents had supplied him he naturally selected first the name of the firm which
was the best known in Blackhampton, and
one the reputation of which was undeniable.
Here, however, he was doomed to receive
further rebuff and disappointment, which was
to be felt by him, too, all the more keenly because not only his feelings but his pocket also
were now involved. He was received cour-
teously, but the verdict upon the " Patent
Archimedian Self-Actor " was much the same
as that which Mr. —— had passed upon it.
They admitted that it was ingenious, but
condemned it as being not more serviceable
than other corkscrews, and much too expensive to be brought into general use. They
told him frankly that they could not think of
taking it up, and most strongly advised him
on no account to spend more money upon it.

With a weary and anxious heart the poor
inventor went to the next on his list, to the
next, and to the next, with varying results;
but though now and again he would be
buoyed up with a favourable opinion, he
never met with anything which he could
call success.

Some would admire it greatly, would predict for it a very large sale, but would regret that "at the present time their house was not in a position to take it up." Some would even half pledge themselves to do so, but must keep it a day or two to consult an absent partner—on whose return a polite letter, declining it, would be sent. Some would be downright rude over it, some jocose, some insulting; but none would undertake its introduction, or offer anything for it.

Heartrending as was the disappointment of all this, it is a singular fact that Gerald, instead of becoming himself disgusted and dissatisfied with his invention, became at each succeeding rebuff more wrapt up in it, more blind to its defects, and more fascinated with its merits. As if it had been in reality a child of his own, he seemed, as it were, for the very sake of his poor corkscrew to grow indignant with its detractors, and over and over again he declared to himself that, in spite of the obtuseness of those to whom he had shown it, it must and should succeed. Like many other unfortunate inventors have done before him, he became infatuated with his production, and as he grew weary and almost ill with defeat, infatuation began to make him reckless.

This was his frame of mind when he called one day upon a manufacturer, who passed a decidedly favourable opinion upon it.

"My dear sir," said he, "this is capital; this will do—this is what we have been wanting for some time. You've got a small fortune here."

"Thank God!" ejaculated Gerald involuntarily, "I've found some one to appreciate it at last!"

"At last? Then I'm not the first you've shown it to?"

"No, you are not. I don't wish to be anything but straightforward with you, and I may as well tell you at once that I've shown it to dozens, who condemn it as though it were dirt."

"You're very outspoken for an inventor, Mr. Triptree. May I ask the names of those who condemn it?"

Gerald produced and handed to him his list; and the manufacturer, who was a rather handsome-looking, very showily-dressed man, pushing the hat which he wore on to the back

of his head, and tilting the office-stool upon
which he sat, glanced through it, and having
glanced, laughed aloud.

" And these all condemn it, do they ?" he
asked merrily.

" All," said Gerald gloomily."

" Why, of course they do, Mr. Triptree!
Now, look here, this house, and this, and this"
ticking them off with a pencil), " are old-
fashioned slow-coaches, who on principle
wouldn't take up a new thing—no, not if
they could make a fortune out of it; this,
this, and this, are already working patent
corkscrews, and couldn't negotiate for a new
one, though I don't doubt they were wild
when they saw yours; half a dozen I see
here are crippled for capital, and couldn't
offer you anything for it, so, as a matter of
course, find fault. I'll bet a five-pound note,
Mr. Triptree, that I could name the correct
reason why each one of 'em wouldn't have anything to say to it, and I'll bet another that it
wasn't because of any fault in the thing itself !"

" Oh, dear !" said Gerald with a sigh of intense relief; " I wish I had come to you
at first !"

" Sir to you," said the manufacturer, touching his hat. " You're very good, I'm sure.
And now what's to be done ?"

" Well, I hope you will take it up."

" Well, as far as I can, I shall only be too
glad : that is, providing we can come to terms.
Let's see.   I believe I'm speaking to the son
of Mr. Triptree, of The Shrubs."

"Yes : I am his eldest son."

" Dear me !   You're a lucky gentleman,
Mr. Triptree—a very lucky gentleman.   I
wish I were the eldest son of such a father.
You would not see me *here* much longer, I
can tell you !   You'll excuse me mentioning
the matter, I'm sure ; but, as a business man,
I like to know who I'm talking to.   Well,
now, with regard to this corkscrew.   I'm your
man, and yet I'm not your man.   I can make
'em for you as well as any one, and I could
sell a lot of 'em, but you see a thing like this
wants universal pushing, and I don't send out
travellers.   Now, supposing I made 'em, and
sold all I could (and I could, no doubt, do a
good thing in 'em), you want some good pushing man to devote his time, or at least a portion of his time, to going round with it, and

making a specialty of it. What a thing of this sort wants, Mr. Triptree, is a start; your ordinary commercial won't bother himself about a new thing, and the trouble it takes to explain it; but only let a good, cute man who is interested in an article, set the ball rolling, and directly the demand 's made, every commercial on the road jumps at the chance of carrying it."

"Then what should you advise me to do?"

"Well, speaking as man to man, and without prejudice or offence, I should ask you, Are you above giving the thing a start yourself? Who is so likely to make a thing go as the man who has invented it, and has its interest most at heart? There's no doubt about it, Mr. Triptree, that if you would condescend to play the commercial for a month or two, the affair would soon be floated, and no factor would travel without it.

"Well," said Gerald honestly; "I tell you frankly that I don't mind what I do to make the thing a commercial success. But how do you propose that I should be paid?"

"Simple enough. You must give me a

sample order of a sufficient quantity to enable
us to produce them at a good selling price,
these you will sell off as samples ; then, the
thing being fairly started, I shall agree to
pay you a royalty on all that I make. But
nothing can be done, sir, until the ground is
laid, and no one can lay it so well as yourself."

"Then I'll lay it!" said Gerald stoutly.
"If energy on my part can secure success, the
thing is half done!"

"Well said, sir ; and they shall be put in
hand at once. Now how many shall we say
for samples ?"

"Well," said Gerald thoughtfully, "I
suppose about five or six dozen would be
plenty."

"Five or six dozen," said the manufacturer in amazement. "Good Lord, Mr.
Triptree; how far would five or six dozen
corkscrews go to supply the population of
England? Five or six thousand would be
nearer the mark ; and then you'd fall short
of it!"

"But—pardon me if I am not very formal,
I am not used to business transactions—for

this first lot I should, I presume, have to pay
you ; and that would involve a greater outlay
than I had anticipated."

" Yes; certainly I should expect to be
paid, but royalties would knock a big figure
off the account; and then, of course, you'd
sell at a profit. So you see in reality no
outlay whatever is required."

"But," said Gerald, "I feel bound to look
at every side of the question. And, supposing
that the thing was a dead failure, and no one
would have anything to say to it, why, then,
I should be left with any quantity of corkscrews on my hands."

The manufacturer gave Gerald a look in
which disgust was mingled with pity.

" Mr. Triptree," he said, " I took you for a
man of spirit. When you came into my office
I said to myself, ' Here, unless I'm very much
mistaken, is a man who'll back his fancy.'
Why, sir, do you think that a thing like
that's going to fail ? Can't you see yourself
that it's a thing that's wanted, and that when
they know where to get it, the public *will*
have it ? Why the very fact of the folks
you've shown it to having declined it as they

did, ought to be sufficient for you. Won't
they just boil over when they see it in the
market?"

"And they *shall* see it in the market!"
cried Gerald, goaded by the recollection of
his recent and repeated snubbings. " I *will*,
as you say, 'back my fancy.' Will you make
one thousand for me?"

"Yes," was the reply. " It ought to be
five thousand; but, as I know there'll soon
be a repeat, 1 don't object to booking your
order for a thousand."

"Thank you. Then please to get them
done as soon as possible. And now with
regard to the price——"

" That, sir, you must leave entirely to me.
Until we come to make them, it's impossible
to quote. You may rely upon it, sir, that
you're in good hands ; and that, though they'll
be turned out well, they'll be turned out at
a figure that will astonish you."

" Still, I should like to have some idea.—"

" Better not ask for it, sir. If you insist, I
must say something that would cover the
very outside of everything; and it wouldn't
be fair to me. You leave it in my hands,

and you may depend I'll do the right thing by you."

And so Gerald "left the matter in his hands," and returning home told Kate that the "Patent Self-Acting Archimedian Corkscrew" was fairly launched at last, and that they might safely look forward to days of affluence.

Pending the production of the corkscrews, several matters of moment occurred in his little family circle.

Hammond Rockcliffe having at length completed the work which had taken him to London, returned to Blackhampton, and, it is needless to say, at once sought an interview with Minnie.

This took place in Mrs. Tryan's little parlour, which, however, was no longer occupied by that estimable mother, she, poor soul, being, through ill-health, now completely confined to her own room.

"Well, Minnie," said Hammond, "again my time of probation is at an end; my stay and my work in London are finished: and now how are you going to reward me for my patience?"

"Ah, how?" said Minnie, "that is the question; the question which, do what I will, I cannot answer. I do not know what would really be your reward, or how your happiness is the likeliest to be secured."

"I do not understand you, Minnie. Surely you do not doubt my steadfastness of purpose?"

"No, I do not; although (for news from London to Blackhampton travels quickly) I believe you were not while you were in London absolutely pining."

"Pining? Certainly I was not pining. It is not in my nature to pine, but to try and make the best of things. I do not know what the news of which you speak may be, but I certainly gave you credit for being superior to those who revel and believe in commonplace gossip."

"And now you find you are mistaken? You see how little, after all, you know of me. Do you not think you would do well to know me better before you press me for my answer?"

"Minnie! Why do you treat me in this way? Is it possible that you—you whom I have judged to be the most simple, single-hearted girl whom I ever knew, are after all but a shallow coquette playing with my feelings? Surely *you* attach no value to idle reports? Why, if I had done the same, I should have believed what I have lately been as good as asked to believe, namely, that you were in my absence encouraging the attentions of another lover!"

" Oh! Then you are not altogether free from the influence of gossip?"

" No; perhaps I am not!"

And so these two, each of whom had aimed at being somewhat superior to the ordinary run of young people, gradually drifted into a commonplace lovers' quarrel! Both, however, felt suddenly the folly of it, and after a pause, Hammond said, in a changed voice :

" Whatever may pass between us, Minnie, do not let us be foolishly angry with each other. Why should we any longer beat about the bush? You have now had plenty of time in which to consider well my offer to you, and I have now a right to demand an answer. What is my answer to be?"

Minnie paused for a few moments, and then, in a voice scarcely audible, said falteringly :

"Mamma is so ill, that I cannot give you my answer now.   Will you wait——-"

" No," said Hammond, firmly ; " I will wait no longer.   You must by this time know your own mind, and whether you do or do not love me, as I love you.   You must give me your answer now."

"Then my answer must be no," said Minnie very quietly, but quite firmly and distinctly.   " You had indeed better have my answer now, and my answer must be no."

And then suddenly breaking down, she said, sobbing :

" Oh, Hammond, do not hate me !"

" I can never hate you," said Hammond. " God only knows how I ever came to be so mistaken in you."

And then he rose to go.   Half-way towards the door, however, he turned and hesitated, as though he would have spoken again.   Minnie, though she did not look up, knew that he did so, and that the next moment must decide her fate.   Had he spoken to her then, she would assuredly have given way, and flinging her resolutions and misgivings to the winds, would have thrown herself into his arms, con-

fessing for him the depth of her love. More
than once he was about to speak, but words,
both of love and of reproach, failed him;
and, without doing so, he abruptly left the
room.

And then Minnie knew that she had sacri-
ficed her life's happiness, and strong of purpose though she was, sobbed her poor heart
out.

But Hammond was sick at heart too, and
withal disgusted with women, and angry with
himself for having a second time in his life
staked his happiness upon feminine caprice.
Indeed, his fortunes as a lover had been unlucky, and having now failed where he had
felt so certain of success, it is not a thing at
which to wonder that he blamed himself for
not having profited by his first hard lesson.
Indeed, he blamed himself more than he did
Minnie, and that not so much because of what
he could not but term her fickleness, but on
account of his own folly in having, notwithstanding his early experience, ever thought
that happiness in a woman's love was to be
found for him.

But though he was inclined to regard

Minnie with contempt rather than with indignation, he could not, being human, help,
when he thought of the successful Blackhampton gentleman (for he of course thought
that Groutage had robbed him of her affection), being very wrath with her.

In this spirit he abruptly left Mrs. Tryan's
house and took lodgings for himself elsewhere,
pursuing his old occupations, but doing his
work listlessly, and feeling in it that all his
old interest had gone.

Not without truth it is said, that for one
who is overwhelmed with disappointment and
sorrow, there is no remedy like that of a sepa-
rate anxiety and the necessity for active work,
and from this point of view it was, for poor
Minnie, well, perhaps, that she should at this
time be occupied with the trouble of the
serious form which her mother's illness had
now assumed.

Never had parent a more patient, gentle,
untiring nurse than Minnie now became ; and
never did mother more gratefully acknowledge
a daughter's tender and loving care than,
with a nature softened by much suffering and
the consciousness that she must soon die, did
Mrs. Tryan.

In little more than a month after Hammond
Rockcliffe made his last appeal, this part of
Minnie's duties came to an end, and the poor,
worldly, arrogant, yet well meaning mother,
lay quietly in her grave.

It was on the very day of her funeral, and
on returning home from it, that Gerald found
Auracaria Villa overwhelmed with packing
cases containing his thousand corkscrews.
There were cases in the unused stable and
coach-house, cases in the little back-yard and
in the entrance hall. To open one of these,
and to produce from it a specimen of the
" Patent Archimedian," was the work of a
very few moments, and in spite of the solem-
nity of the day, and of the ceremony in which
he had just taken part, he could with difficulty conceal his delight at the matured evidence of his ingenuity. He would have been
glad if his wife had seemed more interested in
the matter, and if she would have entered
more heartily into his schemes for the immediate introduction of his patent ; but Kate's
mind was at the present time wholly centred
upon the devising and ordering of expensive
and elaborate mourning, which, notwithstand-

ing the fact that they were now in exceedingly
straightened circumstances, she deemed it
necessary to have. Minnie, who had come to
stay with them, certainly showed some little
sympathy in his plans, but she was evidently
out of health as well as sad at heart, and so
Gerald had to enjoy his enthusiasm all alone.
His intense delight was certainly somewhat
damped when, on the following morning, he
received the manufacturer's account, and found
that, the corkscrews being charged at nine-
and-ninepence each, he had incurred a debt of
little short of five hundred pounds! But
though at first this quite appalled him, his
faith in the success of his invention soon reas-
sured him, and he only bestirred himself the
more to commence, with as little delay as possible, his task of making it known to the public.

But before he was able to do this, he had
another and a harder blow, which came in the
form of a letter from the manufacturer, who
said " that he had unexpectedly met with
heavy and severe losses," and that as he had
" pressing engagements to meet," he should
" esteem it a great favour " if Gerald would
settle his account !

Post-haste Gerald repaired to his office, and without the slightest attempt at disguise, told him frankly that he had not got the money, but that he relied upon the sales of the cork-screws to pay for them.

"It was very unlucky," the manufacturer said. "Of course he was not anxious about the safety of the money, because he knew he was dealing with a gentleman, and because it would take a very short time to turn the corkscrews into cash; but his immediate wants were so urgent that he really should have to press for a settlement."

"But I tell you it is impossible !" said Gerald, in despair. "I have not so much money of my own anywhere !"

"It is very unfortunate," said the manufac-turer again. "Certainly I did not stipulate that it should be a cash transaction, though, knowing who you were, I always felt that it would be so, and at the time when you first came to me I was in a position to give any amount of credit; but as I tell you, Mr. Trip-tree, I'm driven into a regular corner, and can't wait."

"But you'll *have* to wait !" said Gerald,

desperately. "I tell you I *cannot* pay you yet !"

"Oh come, Mr. Triptree! You mean to say that it isn't quite convenient to pay me yet, and I'm sure I'm very sorry to put a gentleman like you to any inconvenience; but of course I know that if you applied to your respected father——"

Gerald flushed crimson, half with anger and half with dismay.

"But I do not mean to apply to my father," said he; "this is my own private business, and will be privately settled. I tell you again that you will have to wait for your money until I have had time to do something with the corkscrews."

"Mr. Triptree," said the manufacturer, "I should be very sorry to annoy you, but I am in immediate want of money, and if you decline to apply to Mr. Triptree, senior, and can suggest no other means of paying me, I · must do so myself."

For the moment Gerald was inclined to curse the unlucky day upon which the idea of the "Patent Archimedian Corkscrew" had entered into his head, so thoroughly dismayed

was he at the position in which he suddenly
found himself. The thought that his father
would come to know of his reckless enterprise
was most horrible to him, for Mr. Triptree
had always sneered at his son's inventive pro-
clivities, and would certainly have regarded
the idea that anything was to be made out of
the unfortunate corkscrew with unmitigated
contempt. A short time ago, when he had
believed him to be immensely wealthy, it
would have been bad enough to have had
such a matter brought before him; but at
the present time, when he was smarting
under the mortification of large monetary
losses, when he had so recently stated that
he must cut off all extraneous expenses, and
when he was growling over every guinea with
which he parted, Gerald felt that such an
ordeal would be unendurable !

It was not that he had intended to deceive
his father, but, knowing well that not only
would he fail to appreciate his invention, but
that he would also be very harsh with him
for having wasted his time upon such
" foolery," he had decided to let him know
nothing of it until he was in a position to

prove that the work of his brain had put money in his pocket.

Than such a catastrophe he felt that any alternative was preferable ; but the manufacturer was obdurate in his demands, and it was not until after a long and agonising discussion that Gerald left him, having undertaken that he would within ten days pay him in hard cash one hundred and fifty pounds, and for the remainder of the debt give him two promissory notes to fall due at different periods.

Concerning the last named Gerald felt little anxiety ; by the time that they would have to be met his invention would be well before the public, and he would be deriving profit from his sales ; but concerning the one hundred and fifty pounds which he was to pay immediately he was at his wit's end. Calculating all his resources he believed that he might be able, by hook and by crook, to raise fifty pounds ; but what of the remaining hundred ?

Clearly there was not sufficient time in which to sell corkscrews to that amount, and there was nothing for it but to borrow. But of whom to borrow ?

One by one he put aside the names of all his friends. Some, he knew, could not help him ; many, he knew, would not ; most, he felt sure, would, if asked, immediately make it their business either directly or indirectly to let his father know what he was doing. He put them all aside until he thought of Hammond Rockcliffe, and then he paused.

That Hammond would if asked help him, if he could, he felt certain, and looking at the fact that his recent employment in London must have put him in receipt of ready money, it seemed likely that he would be in a position to do so ; or even putting that on one side it appeared to him hardly likely that a man of Hammond's connections would have difficulty in raising such a sum as a hundred pounds.

A few months ago he would, had he been in a similar strait, have gone to him at once ; but lately the two friends had seen but little of each other, and somehow, though nothing had been said, an estrangement between them seemed to have grown up.

Now Gerald was conscious that this was mainly due to a feeling which he himself had

that Hammond had not behaved properly
to Minnie ; he had not failed to notice the
attention which at one time his friend had
paid to his sister-in-law, and it was equally
apparent to him that she had regarded him
with more than ordinary favour.   In his own
mind he had quite decided that they were to
marry each other, and than such a union
nothing would have pleased him better, for
he both liked and admired Hammond, as well
as loved and honoured Minnie, while the two
seemed so admirably adapted the one to the
other.   Of Mrs. Tryan's talk on the subject
to his wife, and of her lecture to Minnie, he
knew nothing ; and though for reasons of his
own he preserved a strict silence, he felt
certain that time would bring them together.
When, therefore, after Hammond's return from
London he suddenly gave up his rooms in
Mrs. Tryan's house, and paid Minnie no more
attention than if she had been a most ordinary
acquaintance, he was not only disappointed,
but inclined to be angry, for he could only
think that he had been mistaken in the man,
and that what he had believed in him to have
been a serious attachment, was nothing more

than a most culpable flirtation, concerning which he would have dearly loved to have had his say.

Like his friend the manufacturer, however, he had now "pressing engagements to meet," and felt that he could not afford to indulge in such luxuries as pride or delicacy; so going at once to Hammond's lodgings, and finding him alone in his dingy room, he said with a burning face :

" Rockcliffe, I have come to ask a very great favour of you. I want to borrow one hundred pounds."

" Then you couldn't have come to a better man," said Hammond. " For the first time in my life I've been fool enough to save some money, and was wondering what on earth to do with it when you came in."

" Well that's pleasant hearing, at all events !" said Gerald, with a great sigh of relief. "' You mean you were wondering how you should invest your money ? I can offer you no security but my word ; but I will pay you proper interest."

" My dear Gerald, I should have thought that you knew me well enough to be aware that I know nothing of securities or interest. There's more than a hundred pounds lying in my desk, and if any or all of it is of any use to you, pray have it."

" A hundred pounds at the present time will be of the utmost use to me, and I thank you with all my heart. But why do you speak so carelessly of your money ? Before you went to London your one talk was of thrift."

" Because I'm like a child, Gerald, who has saved up his money for a certain purpose, and finding he can't get what he wants would rather spite himself by throwing his money into the mud than buy anything else."

" I don't understand you," said Gerald.

" And you had better not try, for I certainly cannot understand myself. You know the old saying that a burnt child dreads the fire ? Well can you understand a burnt child being such a fool as to go and deliberately scorch itself? No, you cannot ; but I am in that absurd position, and the new burns have opened up all the old wounds, so that I resemble nothing so much as our old friend the bear with the sore head."

"Oh, Rockcliffe, I don't like to hear you talk like that! Can I do anything for you?"

"Nothing, Gerald. I'm a physician, and I must heal myself. See here is the money. My purpose for it has vanished into thin air, and it cannot do better than help you."

"You do not know what a help it is. Let me tell you what it is for. You remember my old inventions, and how you used to warn me about them? well at last——"

"No, don't tell me what it is for," said Hammond, interrupting him, "because I might warn you again, and then you would think I did not want to let you have the money. But as a general rule I would warn you, unless you can afford to fling money to the winds, to beware of inventions, as I mean to beware of—well, never mind what. How is Mrs. Triptree?"

"She is pretty well. Of course Mrs. Tryan's death has been a trouble both to her and to Minnie."

"Naturally. Is Miss Tryan with you?"

"No. I do not wonder that you ask, for my house is now her natural home; but, with her old obstinacy, she declines to fall

in with other people's views, and only to-day
she has left us.   She has taken lodgings with
a very respectable family, and, to my wife's
great annoyance, has resumed her work as a
gold chain maker."

"I admire her for it," said Hammond.

"Gone back to the old place," he said to
himself when he was alone; "gone back to be
near to my gentlemanly rival probably. Bah!
what a fool I am to think of the girl!—what
a fool ever to have thought of her!"

CHAPTER III.

TEMPTATION.

LIVING by himself in his lonely lodgings, and as much as possible excluding himself from society, Hammond Rockcliffe, as he brooded upon his misfortunes, threatened to become as moody and morose as in his earlier days, and when he was smarting under his first disappointment.

He still continued his work, and to a certain extent kept up in it his old interest and perseverance; but from its practice all pleasure had gone, and, though he laboured conscientiously, it was as one who had no goal to gain, and who toiled rather as a matter of necessity than from a sense of duty.

As much as he could he avoided his old friends, while of making new acquaintances he was very chary, so that his life became indeed a solitary one, until, like all things which are put on one side out of use, he bid fair to become in very truth useless.

That his fate seemed to be an unhappy one was a matter beyond a doubt. Without near relatives or intimate friends, he was, of all others, the very man who required the sympathy and companionship of a wife ; but he was not the man who would marry for marrying's sake, or unless he could see in his bride his ideal of womanhood. Twice had he loved, and twice had he been encouraged to love, and twice he had had his hopes scattered to the winds. Little wonder, then, that he became gradually a misogamist, and felt that, since no one was by his existence directly benefited, the more he kept himself to himself, the better, both for himself and for the community at large, it would be.

He was in this frame of mind, and living after this manner, when, a few months after Minnie had given him her final answer, he received from Percy the following letter :

"Wimpole Street, 11th ——, 187 —.

" DEAR HAMMOND,

" You have ever shown yourself to be so entirely ignorant as to the ways of the world, and so blind as to the manner in which things with me have lately been going, that I am induced to believe that this letter will not only cause you much trouble, but also considerable astonishment.

" That it is not a very pleasant task for a man to sit down and make a written confession that he is an unmitigated blackguard you will readily understand, but that recent events have made me so utterly hardened and indifferent that I feel little or no shame in writing it, will no doubt surprise you.

" In plain English, however, these are the things which I have to tell you, and you will very soon perceive that I have, unfortunately, been the means of making you, to a great extent, a partner in my shortcomings.

" I am an utterly ruined man. I have spent every shilling which I have, or ever had, of my own in the world, and I have spent every shilling which Northover gave to

my wife, and of which he made you and me
co-trustees.

" The letter which I was supposed to have
received from Northover, and on the strength
of which you were induced to sell out my
wife's property, and to entrust it to me for
re-investment, was a forgery. I enclose it
with this, and you will see that it is a good
one. It of course carries with it my con-
demnation, but it may be useful to you as a
proof of the manner in which you were so
easily duped ; for believe me when I say that
I am truly sorry for you, and would gladly
spare you the mortification which, knowing
you, I know you will feel.

" I fancy I see you cursing yourself for
your shortsightedness and folly—and that
you were a fool is a matter beyond doubt ;
but I do not think that in the long run it
would have made much difference, for, one
way or another, I was bound to go to the
devil.

" You will probably marvel that I managed
to get through so large a sum of money in so
short a period of time, but you may accept
my assurance that when a man bets all day,

plays cards one half the night, and dice the other half, and when he has in everything one continuous run of the devil's own luck, the feat is a very simple one.

"Indeed, I have not only got through all the money, but I am also involved in considerable debt, and it is that which has brought matters to a climax.

"Now I need hardly say that I do not make this very plain-spoken, or rather written, confession except on the eve of my relieving my native country of my presence. By the time you get this I shall be far enough away, and very shortly after, all that I have left in the world (which consists almost solely of furniture upon which there is a bill of sale) will be seized and confiscated.

"Now, my object in writing all this to you is that I think it is only fair to you that you should hear the miserable truth directly from me, and also that I may say a word to you on behalf of my unfortunate wife.

"It is impossible that she should go with me. When she knows what I have done she will hate me, and my pride would not allow me, after she knows all, to humiliate myself

before her. Our marriage has been all along
a mistake. I never succeeded in making her
happy, and lately I have made her thoroughly
unhappy; so that in reality she will be better
without me.   I leave her, however, with
hardly a friend in the world. It would be
idle to expect that my father's family will do
anything for her, and as I believe that she
has relatives whom you know, and to whom,
until her father can be communicated with,
she will probably apply for shelter, I have, in a
letter which I have written and shall leave for
her, recommended her to apply to you for advice.

" You will not, I am sure, refuse it. You
once cared for her, and it is a pity for her
sake, poor child, that she did not marry you
instead of me.

" I shall say no more. It would be a
mockery for me to express regrets or to promise amendment. Bad in my case will, if a
worse can be found, undoubtedly go to worse;
and when the worse is at its worst, and I am
driven by extremity to make an end of an
unlucky existence, no one need mourn me.

"""Yours,

" PERCY ROCKCLIFFE."

As Hammond read this letter his heart seemed to stand still ; he was, in very truth, aghast—aghast at the sudden light which was thrown upon Percy's character—aghast at the enormity of the sins which had been committed, and aghast at his own position ; for was not he, in his capacity as trustee, equally responsible with Percy for the safety of Gertrude's money? The letter, too, was written with such amazing coolness, it seemed to treat of everything which had been done as such a matter of course, that it had the effect of making him feel that he, in his culpable carelessness, had been quite as much, if not even more, to blame than his abandoned cousin ; and he immediately began to fulfil Percy's prophecy, and fell to cursing himself for his negligence and folly.

Curse as he would, however, he could not alter what had been done, nor could the remorse of a lifetime alleviate the misery which had befallen poor Gertrude. When he thought of her—robbed of her money, deceived and deserted by her husband, friendless and practically fatherless—when he thought of the time when he was in London, and how Percy

had cheated and cajoled both himself and her
—when he thought of her in days gone by, a
sweet and loving girl, he ground his teeth in
rage, and for the moment felt that the only
thing in life which could at that moment give
him any satisfaction would be a personal encounter with the author of this poor girl's
ruin.

And what ought he to do? The letter
told him that by this time Gertrude herself
probably knew the worst, and that the
only advice which her absconding husband
had left her was that she should apply to him
for advice! And he was responsible for at
least one half of her misfortunes! For, in
his agony, Hammond was inclined to class
his own reprehensible carelessness alongside
with Percy's outrageous felony.

His first impulse was to go to Gertrude and,
confessing his fault, to do all that a man could
for that poor outcast; but in this he was re-
strained, by his doubt as to his own position,
for, in his ignorance, he did not know how
far he himself might for the defalcation in his
trust be amenable to the law, and whether,
as a man, who had undoubtedly been greatly

at fault, but who still was one who wished to maintain his honour untarnished, it did not behove him at once to surrender himself.

And yet the thought of Gertrude, in her distress, so moved him, that he was ever on the point of going to her, and was only deterred by the fear that she would now only look upon him as the unfaithful guardian of her fortune,—nay, might even suspect (as undoubtedly would the rest of the world), that he had, with Percy, benefited by her losses.

And so throughout the entire day Hammond remained in doubt and dismay, merely reading Percy's dreadful letter over and over again, and remaining wholly undetermined upon any line of action. What seemed to him most probable was, that Gertrude would at once apply to her uncle, Anthony Northover, who would, of course, take immediate steps to discover the whereabouts of his brother, who (even if he did nothing worse), would cover him with reproaches and steep him in humiliation.

And did he not deserve reproaches? Was it not right that he should suffer humiliation? Unwittingly and unwillingly he had done a griev-

ous wrong to those whom he would have
served most faithfully, and as the betrayer of
the trust which had been reposed in him could
expect from Gertrude and her father nothing
but indignation and aversion.

Oh, how sad it was to him to think that
Gertrude, whom he had once loved so fondly ;
in whose companionship he had but lately
taken such delight, and whom he had endeavoured so loyally to aid, should think of
him as a traitor, and deem his past conduct
as part of a basely-designed scheme !

No, he must not go to Gertrude. Though
he might still devote his life to efforts to
make her reparation, he could never, he felt,
go to her again.

But late that night, Gertrude came to him.

He was sitting in his gloomy room brooding, as he had all day brooded, over these
things when the street door bell was rung.
Like many bachelors who are without the
means of obtaining feminine advice and assistance, Hammond, when he had found it
needful to go lodging-hunting, had taken the
first rooms which came in his way without
much eye to their comfort, or many questions

as to his prospects of being well cared for. His choice had been an unlucky one, for though they cost him as much money as really good lodgings should have done, they were dark, ill-furnished, badly situated, and the attendance for which he was exorbitantly charged was, in reality, no attendance at all. These things, however, had not greatly troubled him, and he made himself easy with the reflection that, all lodgings were very much the same, and that to be free from the frequent visits of an inquisitive and communicative landlady, and from the attendance of a slatternly servant girl, were, after all, advantages. The doing of the general work of the house, however, was another matter, and when the street door bell had rung for the third time, and he was by that fact apprised that he was alone in the house, it was not without annoyance that he rose to answer it.

The shock which, when he saw Gertrude there, he experienced, was but a repetition of the shock which her husband's letter had that morning given him.

"Good God!" he ejaculated, and led her to his room.

Then Gertrude, looking at him wildly, and holding up to him her hands imploringly, said.

"Oh, Hammond, do not turn me away! Do, oh do, be kind to me!"

"Kind to you?" said Hammond. "I, kind to you, who have ruined you? I, who could not have done you greater injury had you been my enemy? You could hardly have come to a worse person for kindness, Gertrude."

"Do you know what has happened?" she asked.

"I do. This morning I received from Percy, from your husband, and,—curse him— my cousin, a letter, in which he told me what he had done, and how he had left you."

"And did he tell you that I was to come to you?"

"He told me that he advised you to do so; but oh, Gertrude, you cannot think that it is well to follow the advice of such a man as that!"

"I do not come because he advised me, although he did so. I come because, directly I realised this awful trouble, my heart turned to you. Oh, Hammond! you are the only friend I have. I believe that except my poor mother, and, after his manner, my father, you are the only human being who ever really cared for me. In days gone by, and when I did not know its worth, you gave me your love ; oh in pity's sake do not turn from me now, now when I am nearly mad with terror and with misery !"

" Gertrude," said Hammond, in a broken voice : " it is evident that you do not know all, or that knowing you do not realise. I, Gertrude, I whom you call your only friend, am almost as much to blame for your misfortunes as your wretched husband. The money which your father——"

Gertrude laughed,—a wild hysterical laugh —" Money !" she cried derisively. " Money ! What is money to the trouble which has torn my heart ever since I have been married ! What is money to those who thirst for love ! I never wanted money ; without money I was strong and happy ; since I have had it I have been weak and miserable. Money broke down my poor father, and it was for money that Percy married, deceived, and has forsaken me. Thank God that the wretched money has gone !"

" But Gertrude, those who have money entrusted to them as I had——"

" Oh Hammond !" she interrupted him, "you do not think that I could for one moment wrong you with a suspicion of having betrayed your trust ? No. I never could have done so, even if my wicked husband had not in the letter which he left, told me how he had cheated you, how he had forged a letter, and, because you believed him to be as honest and as good a man as yourself, had brought great trouble upon you. Hammond, if for no other reason, I ought to be here tonight to beg your forgiveness for the sorrow, which through me and mine, has come to you."

He was deeply moved, and could only say, falteringly :

" Would to God, Gertrude, that I could think you would in this dreadful business always think the same of me !"

" I shall ever think the same of you," she said.

" This, Gertrude, I swear to you—that while God gives me the strength to work, you shall never want ; an objectless life shall be devoted, heart and soul, to one object— the reparation of a broken trust, and the devotion of myself to your service. I did not for one moment, Gertrude, think that you would come to me, and not knowing what you might think of me, I dared not come to you. I thank Heaven that you came, I thank Heaven and you for your sweet forgiveness. Where I saw nothing but darkness I see light, and, in the light, what I may yet be able to do for you. Come, Gertrude, I will take you to your relations."

But Gertrude shrank from him.

"What do you mean?" she said, in a frightened voice.

"Your Uncle Anthony lives near here. For the present you had better go to him, and no doubt your cousins——"

"Oh, no, no, no, no!" she cried. "I would rather die than go, in my grief and my humiliation, to them. I would rather kill myself than go to them. Hammond, I have been so wretched lately, that I have often thought that I *would* kill myself. Last night, when this great and horrible trouble came, I almost *tried* to kill myself; but I am not a brave or strong woman, Hammond, I am only a poor weak creature ; I cling to life, and I am afraid to die. But I would rather die. I would rather kill myself than go to people who would despise me and who would not love me. You think I do not know what I am saying ; but I do. You do not know what I have been suffering lately. Percy has been cruel—oh, so cruel to me ; and my love has dried up with loneliness and fear ; and one night he—he struck me, Hammond, and then my heart turned to stone towards him, and my love went away. And now he has left me, and for that—oh God, forgive me !—I am glad."

"My poor Gertrude !—my poor, poor child! But what are you to do ?"

"To stay with you ! Oh, Hammond, let me stay with you ! I do not mind what I do —anything ; but let me stay with you ! You will love me, I know. You will be good and gentle with me ; in everything I know I can trust you—oh, so well. See here ! I have a father, but do not know where he is ; and perhaps he is dead. I am friendless, and I am forsaken. What am I, to care what people

say or think ? Whatever I may do, no one
will say a kind word or think a kind thought
of me. Let me stay with you. It is a dreadful thing to say, but I believe you love me,
and that you would have me stay with you."

Sobbing, she flung herself on the floor at
his feet, and he, conscious of a sudden rush of
new thoughts which set every nerve in his
body tingling, leant over her.

Why should it not be as she said ? Could
he not also say, " What was *he* that he should
care what people said or thought of *him* ?"
Almost as friendless as she was herself, had
not circumstance made it the first duty of his
life to work and care for her ; and how could
he so well do it as if he were ever by her
side ? Was she not the first woman whom
he had ever loved ? and would he not, had he
been suffered to do so, have loved her with
the steadfast loyalty of a lifetime ? Was not
that old love, which had for a time slumbered,
now in very pity reawakened, until at this
moment it seemed to burn within him as
strongly as ever it had done ? Who was he,
and what had he done, that throughout his
life he should be denied a woman's love ? He

had loved Gertrude, and had allowed himself
to lose her love ; he had loved Minnie, and,
as it seemed to him, had been deceived by
her.   Why should he not now accept the returned love which was offered him ?   Why
should not they, Gertrude and himself, set
conventionalities at defiance, and be to each
other all in all ?

For what he had done the world would
blame him.   What was the world to him, and
why should it not have real cause to blame
him ?   Forsaken by her husband, Gertrude's
chance of happiness in the world was gone ;
what was it to the world if she endeavoured
to regain happiness by remaining with him ?

Thus thinking, and thus tempted, he said,
as he bent over her :

" Gertrude, my first love, and my darling,
if it is your will to stay with me, I will, while
I have life, never leave you."

And then, still convulsively sobbing, she
rose, and throwing herself into his arms and
clinging closely to him, she said :

" Oh, no ; let me stay with you.   I cannot
die—I am afraid to die ; and without you I
cannot live."

Fervently he kissed her, and yielding to the strength of his temptation, vowed to her, with words of passionate devotion, that he would never leave her more.

But the agitation and distress through which she had passed, and under the effects of which she was labouring, were too much for poor Gertrude, and it was evident to Hammond that his first care for her must be that of a doctor. Suddenly her strength failed her, and from a condition of extreme excitement she fell into a state that bordered on the comatose. She had travelled during the day alone from London, and no food of any sort had passed her lips; her one wild idea had been to come to Hammond, and having satisfied herself that she was sure of his protection, the energy with which she had nerved herself for her journey entirely gave way.

Having prevailed upon her to take a sufficiency of nourishment (Hammond had never before bewailed the limited resources of his establishment), he carried her almost lifeless in his arms to his own room, and there having made her as comfortable as he could, and having assured himself that her exhausted

condition would at least bring to her the re-
freshment of sleep, he came down again to his
sitting-room to reflect on this sudden change
in his affairs, and, if possible, to form plans for
the future.

Throughout the greater part of that night
Hammond paced his room to and fro, revolv-
ing, in a mind almost disordered by the inten-
sity of the day's excitement, his determination
that Gertrude and he should part no more.
He would at once take her away to some place
where neither of them would be known, and
where no one could point at her the finger of
scorn. For immediate necessities he had
money enough, and to spare, and for the rest
he was possessed of strength and knowledge
sufficient to earn for them both a livelihood.
In some distant and well-chosen part of the
world they might well live happily together,
bound to each other by the ties of an early
love, and even more closely by the remembrance of their mutual misfortune.

Ever and anon he flung himself on the sofa,
and for a few moments rested feverishly and
uncomfortably, quickly starting up from a
confused dream to realise the existing state

of affairs, and to fall again to pacing the room ; and more than once he stole upstairs to look at Gertrude slumbering wearily in his bed. It was after contemplating that fair but suffering face, and reflecting upon her weakness as compared with his strength, and that his first duty as her protector should surely be to protect her against herself, that compunctions arose ; but these he put on one side with a stern hand, telling himself that her happiness as well as his lay in their chance of remaining together ; that with what they might choose to do no human being had a right to interfere ; that as soon as to-morrow dawned he should take her away to commence with him a new life, and that if the world chose it might associate their departure together as part of the collapse of his cousin's household.

But when the morrow came it hardly needed Hammond's practised eye to discern that any immediate departure was out of the question, for the agony of mind through which Gertrude had passed had proved too much for her, and when she awoke she was already in a state of high fever, and this hourly increasing, she became within a few hours completely delirious.

This new aspect of affairs presented new difficulties. The fever promised to be in itself a highly dangerous one; the delay in taking Gertrude away from any place in which her identity would be likely to be discovered, was disastrous to Hammond's plans; and the immediate perplexity of accounting to his landlady (who had the night before retired to rest ignorant of the fact that her house contained a new inmate) for the invalid's presence in his room, was a very awkward one.

Much of the making of the future of his own and Gertrude's life depended (though he never knew it) on the few blundering words in which he did this. It seemed to him, however, that the mind of the good lady was, with the assurance which he gave her that all trouble would be handsomely paid for, satisfied; and having engaged a skilled nurse, he devoted himself to a physician's duties.

Poor Gertrude's illness was a very critical one. By anxiety and unhappiness for some time her strength had been undermined, and under the misery and excitement of the collapse in Percy's affairs, her overwrought mind had given way, and for several days she was delirious with brain fever.

It was while watching by her bedside, not knowing whether she would live or whether she would die, and almost inclined to believe that for her an unconscious death would be a boon, that the fever which had raged in Hammond's mind, and under the influence of which he had succumbed to temptation, and allowed sudden desire to usurp the place of honourable doing, abated.

Bitter was the remorse which he now felt, that he should, for one single moment, have allowed himself to think of following a course in which, both for Gertrude and himself, there would have been nothing but a life of dishonour and shame. Agonising were the feelings with which he contemplated her poor, unconscious, suffering face, and with which he had to acknowledge to himself that he had really thought seriously of things of which it was now evident she had spoken while under the influence of an excitement which had terminated in this terrible fever of the brain ; and heartrending as it was to see her suffer,

and to know that if she should recover her
reason and her strength, it would only be to
recognise her unhappy lot, he could not but
thank God that she had been stricken at the
right moment, and before he had so far yielded
to his temptation as to be unable to have re-
traced his steps.

Now, if she should recover, however sad
her life would be, he could still maintain his
own and her honour; he could still toil and
care for her as he would for a dear and unfortunate sister.

He had yet to learn, however, how much
mischief in those few hours, in which he had
allowed himself to give his mind to the allure-
ments of temptation, had been done.   The
right course for him to have pursued on that
night on which Gertrude came to him would
undoubtedly have been to have taken her to
her relatives, and *then* to have commenced on
her behalf that life of self-abnegation and
atonement for the trust which he felt that he
had betrayed, which it was now his desire to
lead.

But, having been tempted, he had allowed
the poor bewildered, irresponsible girl to

remain in his rooms. On the following morning her fever had developed itself and removal was out of the question, and then, instead of going to Anthony Northover and telling him everything, he had foolishly determined (feeling quite confident that her presence in his lodgings would never by them be heard of) to await the issue of her illness, so that her wishes might be consulted.

It so happened, however, that the stream of scandal, which, in spite of all precautions, will always find some leak or cranny through which to trickle, had in this case a clear and well-cut course, leading directly to that very quarter which Hammond would have kept most securely guarded.

The proprietress of his lodgings, who, according to the orthodox tale of lodging-house-keepers, was one who had " seen better days," was, as is often the case with lodging-house-keepers, a widow with a large family, her husband having, after the manner of most defunct husbands of lodging-house-keepers, died, leaving her encumbered, not only with the aforesaid large family, but also with a house which was as much too large for her

requirements as for her means.   To let or
to sell this with its furniture and fixtures
would, of course, have been the most sensible
plan for her to have pursued ; but equally, of
course, she declined to do either, and as a
sailor clings to the last fragment of a wreck,
so she clung to the last record of her better
days, and, notwithstanding the discomfort of
the thing, preferred to live with her large
family in the close kitchen and unwholesome
attics, while her lodgers perpetrated the final
deeds of destruction on her dilapidated furniture, to living in a house which would have been
at once suited to her position and income.

Of the offspring of this good lady, the
majority were " out at service," and it so
chanced that one young damsel was at this
very time a housemaid in the employ of
Anthony Northover, and, as the young Northovers pertaining to this branch of the family
were prone to be on terms of exceeding intimacy with their domestics, it naturally
happened that Hammond Rockcliffe's whereabouts, and, it might almost be said, his daily
doings, were to them thoroughly well-known.

Thus, in the Northover household, the ex-

traordinary arrival of Hammond's "lady friend,"
as poor Gertrude was by the little housemaid
styled, her subsequent illness, and her continued sojourn in his rooms, were facts well
known and freely discussed, and conjectures
concerning her were rife. When, however, Anthony Northover came to hear, as he soon did, of
Percy's downfall, of his debts and of his dis-
appearance, when he was given to understand
that not only his but his wife's money had been
squandered ; when he remembered that Hammond was a party in Gertrude's trust ; and
when he reflected on what, through the agency
of young Fred, he had heard of the recent
intimacy of the cousins in London, and especially of Hammond's constant companionship
with his niece, his suspicions were fully
roused, and he began to think that the whole
affair had been planned between the trustees,
and that the one was as bad as the other ;
and when, therefore, he discovered that Hammond's mysterious " lady friend" was no other
than Gertrude herself, he, to use his own
words, " put this and that together, and saw
the whole thing as clear as noon-day !"

In the meantime, the crisis of Gertrude's

illness had passed, and gradually she became
convalescent. When she first recovered her
consciousness, it seemed as though she could
not remember what had happened, or where
she was, but slowly the recollection of the
dreadful day on which Percy had left her,
and she had fled to Blackhampton, came back
to her, and she again recognised the friendless-
ness and the misery of her lot. To Hammond, however, it was quite evident that she
was entirely forgetful of what she had said
to him on the night when she had come
to him, and that she believed that she was,
when she arrived, already delirious. When
she was sufficiently recovered to talk to him
connectedly he had proof of this in her manifest desire to explain to him the motives
which had induced her to come, which were,
she said, " not only because Percy had advised
her to do so, and that, from that, she thought
he might have some definite plan to suggest
to her, but also because she regarded him as
her only true friend—as the sole being upon
whom she could rely ; and, again, because she
never could have rested until he had had
from her lips the assurance of her conviction

that in the squandering of her money he was wholly blameless, though, like herself, deceived."

Again and again she faltered to him this explanation, regarding him the while with such sweet, pitiful, innocent, and trustful looks, that his heart was torn with anguish, when he thought how, for one brief night, he had been tempted to take advantage of the confidence which she placed in him.

The shock which the poor young creature had suffered had been so heavy an one, and her fever had been so intensely severe, that it was evident that her recovery would be prolonged, and Hammond determined that he could not talk to her about her future prospects until sufficient time had elapsed to make her strong enough to face the difficulties of her position. To place her with her relations was his only idea, and he could not but notice that of all others this would be to Gertrude the most distasteful, for whenever he tried to mention their names she feebly begged "That she might see none of them, but remain with him until her father came home;" and weakly yielding to her wishes, he (having taken care to ascertain that Anthony Northover was as ignorant of Godfrey's whereabouts as he was himself) let matters drift on.

Fortunately his selection of a nurse, who was with her day and night, had been an admirable one, and neither from nurse or doctor could patient have received more careful or considerate attention. When the days on which her life had been in imminent danger had passed, Hammond resumed his wonted work, and that with increased interest and vigour, for once more he felt that he had in his labours an object, and a duty to perform for which the fruit of those labours would be essential.

Soon, however, the day came on which he felt that some decided step must be taken, and that he must make her acquainted with his views. Already she was, for an hour or two in the day, able to be dressed and to sit in an easy-chair, and might very shortly with safety be removed to another house.

" Ah, how he should miss her !" he thought with a sinking heart, as he sat by the side of her chair trying to interest her with trivial conversation, and rather dreading what was to come.

This room of his wore a wonderfully different aspect to that which, when he had been its sole occupant, it had done. It was not one which under any circumstances would have looked very cheerful, but the little feminine nicknacks and luxuries which he had, to make it appear attractive to Gertrude, one by one purchased ; the fresh flowers which it had been his daily task to provide, and above all the traces everywhere of order and of cleanliness, which had arrived with the nurse, had made, by comparison, that which had been as gloomy an apartment as had ever been devoted to the god of sleep, quite a bright and pleasant chamber.

" Gertrude," said Hammond, " can you listen to a little serious talk to-day ?"

" Oh, yes," she said ; " I am getting quite strong now."

" That is right ! Then we must begin to think of what you are to do."

" Of what I am to do ?" she repeated.

" Yes, Gertrude ; in other words of your future life !"

"Oh, Hammond, I wish that I had no future life!"

"No, no; you must not say that; that is not grateful to me who did so much to bring back your life."

"Then I will not say it," she said; "for anything would be worse to me than that you should think me ungrateful."

"Then you must promise me to listen patiently to what I have to say. I have thought so much, Gertrude, of what will be the right thing for you to do, and I can only see one course open."

"And that is?"

"That until your father can be found and communicated with, you must go to your uncle and cousins."

"Oh, Hammond, I cannot!"

"Do not say you cannot, because when I show you that it is your duty, I am sure that you will go."

"But I do not know that they would have me."

"They have good hearts, and will, I am sure, be glad to have you; and you will not be dependent upon them, Gertrude, because

I find that saved from the wreck of your fortune there is a trifle (very little, it is true, but which may by care be made more), which if paid quarterly will, at least, make you independent."

" Oh, I am glad to hear that ! But if that is the case, why cannot I live elsewhere ?"

" No, dear ; I have thought of it all. You are too young and too—too attractive, Gertrude, to live alone ; and it is right that you should be under the care of your own relations. Do not be despondent about it, Gertrude ; I am sure that they will do their best for you, and if they and you will let me, I will, until your father comes back to you, come very very often to see you."

" And when he comes back you will come oftener still ?"

" No, Gertrude ; I shall never come then. How, having betrayed my trust, can I ever meet your father face to face again ?"

" Hammond, you must not say so ! Will he not rather hear from me how nobly, how generously, you have fulfilled your trust ?"

Hammond shook his head in silence. Gertrude leant towards him, and, taking his

strong hand into her thin and almost trans-
parent ones, said :

"Acts, Hammond, speak better than words ;
to show you how implicitly *I* trust you I will,
without another word, act as you think best
for me. Will you go and see my uncle at
once ?"

Thus the thing was settled, and on the
evening of the same day Hammond set forth
for Anthony's house ; and as he approached it
was most disagreeably impressed by the pecu-
liarity of his own position. What would
Gertrude's uncle say to the man who had
allowed her money to be taken from her ? and
what would he think of him for not having
acquainted him earlier with her whereabouts ?
He was soon to know.

He was shown by the servant into the
elaborate drawing-room, which in these days
of prosperity was Mrs. Northover's chief pride,
but which on the present occasion looked, on
account of its being devoid of fire and (with
the exception of one gas burner) of light, as
dreary as most rooms of state, at such times,
do.

Here for a space of ten minutes he was

left to admire the gorgeous satin furniture, the many-coloured carpet, the strikingly bound books, the bewildering (not to say bilious) wall paper, the multifarious ornaments (mostly of cut glass), the enlarged photographic portraits of Mr. and Mrs. Northover and the other members of the family, and the numerous gilt-framed mirrors, with which the room was crowded and its walls decorated.

Then the door opened, and, redolent of the perfume of choice " Havannahs " and hot whisky and water, Anthony Northover confronted him.

" How do you do, Mr. Northover ?" said Hammond, approaching him, and expecting the usual hearty, if over familiar, greeting to which he had been accustomed.

But Anthony's hands remained in his trousers' pockets, and his face wore as stern a look as its easy lines would allow.

" Well," he said, " well, Mr. Rockcliffe, what do you expect me to say to you ? and what do you want with me ?"

" I wanted," said Hammond, reddening and feeling both angry and uncomfortable, " I wanted to talk to you, sir, about many things, of some of which I should from your manner infer that you have already heard, and, having heard, have misjudged me."

" Yes," Anthony answered ; "I have heard one or two things. People who fly their kites as open as you do, Mr. Rockcliffe, can't expect but what they'll be caught at it."

" I am not going to defend myself, Mr. Northover. I have been grossly careless, though God knows my carelessness arose from ignorance rather than from wilfulness. You have heard then, I presume, of my cousin's ruin ?"

" I have heard of his damned roguery, if that's what you call his ruin !"

"I cannot be indignant with you for sub-stituting the word. I do not come here to attempt to excuse either him or myself. I am here to plead the cause of his poor wife."

"What!" cried Northover, looking genuinely astonished. " My God, Rockcliffe, do you mean to tell me that you—*you*—have got the face to come into the house of an honest man, who is her uncle, and to do that !"

" Mr. Northover, what do you mean ?"

" Mean ! Why, I mean what I say. Then

you're tired of her, I suppose, and being tired, want to fling her back on her low-born relatives."

" Mr. Northover, you do not know what you are saying. Do you think—— ?"

" 'Tchah I Do I think ? Don't I know ? Were *you* fool enough to think that you can do as you have done, and not be found out ? I know this, young man, that the night that that poor miserable niece of mine left her husband, or the night he left her, it doesn't matter which, she came to you, and that she's been living with you ever since ; and I know more than that, and that is that if there's a pin to pick between such a pair of d——d scamps as you and your precious cousin, you're the worst of the two !"

" Good Heavens, sir !" cried Hammond, " let me explain !"

" Explain !" returned Northover, who had now worked himself into a towering passion. " What explanation can you give unless you expect me to swallow a parcel of fulsome lies ! There's only one explanation, sir, to a young girl's coming to a man's house and stopping there ; and even if I was fool enough not to know that, haven't I heard from young Fred, that when you were in London, you went about with her so that folks used to say that it was hardly known which of the two was her husband ? It was an evil day for my brother when you two 'gentlemen' came into his house ; between you you've robbed him of his money, you've robbed him of his peace of mind, and you've ruined his poor daughter, and every honest man should cry shame on you !"

Hammond, who had become ashy pale, was so agitated that he could scarcely speak, but after a few moments he said—

" Of course I see the horrible construction which you, and no doubt others, have put upon things, but surely you are open to conviction ? If you will not listen to, or believe me, will you let your niece——?"

" No, no !" said Anthony hurriedly. "Don't send her to me, and don't let her think of coming here. I'm sorry for her, but women are hard about these things, and if Mrs. Northover saw her here, or thought she would try to see our girls, I believe she'd tear her limb from limb ! I've spoken to you plainly and I meant to. What's the use of talking to me of 'conviction,' when the thing's as clear as noonday? You've ruined her, Rock-cliffe! Make the only amends you can by taking her well away from here, and taking good care of the poor thing!"

In his terrible distress and agony of mind, Hammond felt that he could say nothing more, and taking his hat walked to the door; Anthony followed, and opening for him the outer one, let him into the little garden which led to the high road. He had hardly gone a few paces, however, before he was re-called, and Anthony said, in a low voice, and as though fearful of being overheard,—

" Do you want any money for her? That way I'll always help her, but tell her to come to the office, not here, not on any account here : or better still to send me a line to the office. God knows, I'm sorry for the girl!"

" You misjudge both her and me," was all that Hammond said as he went away.

The horror of the situation, now that he fully realised it, was something awful to him, and he felt in a very agony of despair. As much as though he had yielded to the tempta-

tion of that night when Gertrude had, with
frenzied and disordered mind begged that she
might remain with him, he had compromised
both himself and her ; and was it not, alas !
because he had for a time allowed himself to
think of evil things, that all this had come to
pass, for if he had on that night obeyed the
dictates of his conscience, would he not then
and there have taken her to her relatives ?
In a very torment of remorse he remembered,
now that it was too late, how often he had
told himself that this was what he ought to
have done, and how his own momentary passion had overruled his better senses. That
Anthony Northover should, having heard that
Gertrude was with him, think as he did was
a matter of course, and he felt now, as he
had felt when he was with him, that to attempt, even by telling him the simple truth,
to make excuses was idle.

But what was he to do ? To return to
Gertrude, and to let her remain with him,
knowing that the whole world would regard
her with scorn, was something awful to him ;
to tell her that her friends, or those who
should have been her friends, refused to take

her among them, seemed a task impossible
for him to undertake; perhaps the only
course left open to him was really to take her
away with him to some place where both
would be unknown, and yet, now that he saw
things in their true light, such a course seemed
to him to be revolting !

And he had no one to whom to turn for
advice,—no one, except the Anthony Northovers, upon whom he could feel that poor deserted, friendless, Gertrude had any claim !
It did, indeed, seem that he was the one
being upon whom she could depend, and yet
to remain with him would be fatal to her good
name.

Suddenly a thought darted through his
racking brain which, though at first put on
one side as an impossibility, seemed after all
to be the only one which contained any light,
and in the desperation of feeling that he
must immediately do something, he decided
to act upon its sudden impulse.

The thought was that he would go to
Minnie Tryan and ask her to tell him what he
ought to do. Minnie's lodgings were not very
far off, and he at once proceeded to them.

He found Minnie sitting quietly after her day's work, industriously sewing by the light of her shaded lamp, just as she had been wont to do in her mother's parlour on the evenings when he had first learned to love her. She looked just the same Minnie as of old, bright, neat, and cheerful; though when she rose in astonishment at Hammond's unexpected appearance a deep blush was on her face.

"What is the matter?" she asked in alarm. "Have you come to tell me any bad news?"

"No, no," he said to reassure her. "I have come because I want advice, and because I believe that you will be able to give it me."

Minnie smiled as she resumed her seat.

"I am sure I ought to feel grateful to you for thinking so highly of me," she said. "I do not know that I can give advice, but if there is anything in which I can help you, I shall indeed be glad."

"I will tell you," said Hammond.

And then he told the story of Gertrude's married life, feeling sure that Minnie would remember who Gertrude was, and how she had from his own lips heard of his early love

for her; he told her how he had been
Gertrude's trustee, and that through gross
carelessness and ignorance of his duties he
had been a party to the misappropriation and
squandering of her fortune; he told her of
her father's mysterious absence and silence,
and of her husband's desertion of her; of
how she had come to him regarding him as
her only friend; of how she had remained
in his rooms and of her subsequent illness;
and lastly of how the consequence of this
second folly on his part had been to deprive
her not only of the assistance, but even of
the good opinion of her relatives. In short,
he told her all, suppressing only that one
wild thought which in an evil hour he
had, for a short time, allowed himself to
cherish.

"And now what am I to do?" he asked.
" You see that of a great part of her troubles I
have been the main cause, and she, poor soul,
is as friendless as I am."

"Do you ask me for my opinion," said
Minnie.

" Indeed I do."

" Then I think that what she chiefly wants

is the protection and companionship of one of her own sex."

" Just so.　But she has no friends."

" You see, Mr. Rockcliffe, you have unintentionally most grievously compromised the poor girl, and you must not mind me saying that in not at once telling her relatives that she had come to you, you were very much to blame.　No doubt in the distress of the moment you hardly knew what you were doing, but, indeed, you should have known better."

" I know it, and most bitterly regret it; but unluckily I did not do it at the right moment, and then she became delirious, and, thinking that no one would hear of her whereabouts, I decided to do nothing until she could be consulted."

" Yes ; you fell into the common error of believing that because you choose to keep yourself very much to yourself, and know and mix with very few people, that no one knows anything of you or that your affairs are never the subject of discussion, whereas the case is just the reverse.　Why, Mr. Rockcliffe, the fact of poor Mrs. Rockcliffe having arrived at your lodgings, and of her having remained there, was well known within a few days of her coming. I, little as I am in the way of hearing scandal, heard of it some time ago."

Hammond coloured deeply as he said, in a voice which was full of emotion :

"And did you put a wrong interpretation on my conduct and on hers ? Did you think ill of me ?"

"No," said Minnie quietly, but very firmly; "I know you too well to think ill of you. I could see that you were acting unwisely, but of the goodness of your motives I had no doubt."

He looked at her gratefully, but at the same time felt most keenly how unworthy he was of her confidence, how unworthy (alas !) of the love from her which he had hoped to gain !

"And now you want me to tell you what I think you ought to do ?" said Minnie cheerfully. "That her relations here will have nothing to say to her does not in the least surprise me. I have seen something of them, and though Mr. Anthony Northover is a most kind-hearted man, Mrs. Northover and his daughters would, I am sure, be too much

afraid of injuring their own position in what
they call 'society' (and a very poor society it
is), to hold out a helping hand to their poor
cousin now that she is in such trouble. You
say that except these she has no other relatives, and no friends ?"

" Not one. I never knew any one so
friendless. She will have a little money—
only a small sum which has been saved from
the wreck of her property, but still sufficient
for her to live upon."

"And you only want to place her some-
where until her father can be communicated
with, and either be brought home to her, or
direct that she may go to him ?"

" Yes; that is what I want."

" Then do you think she would come to
me? I could engage another room for her
here, you could come and see her and keep a
watch over her, and I should at least be a
companion to her."

" Oh, Minnie, how kind, how good you are !
Of all other things it is what I should most
desire. But—but—have you thought of yourself—of what people might be likely to say ?"

Minnie tossed her head proudly.

"I have never yet, Mr. Rockcliffe, given any one occasion to say unkind things of me, nor do I suppose that I ever shall!"

And then, after a short pause, she added :

"If you really like my plan, go and tell the poor girl of it. Assure her that I will do everything in my power to make her happy, and tell her that if she wishes it I will come to her to-morrow morning, and make all the arrangements for her removal."

"God bless you!" said Hammond, with tears in his eyes. "I can never tell you what I think of your great, great goodness."

And highly though he estimated that goodness, it is probable that, considering the mental effort which it had cost her, he never put a sufficiently high value upon Minnie's present help ; for after his departure, unseen of any, her silent room alone (just as it had been of the torture which she had lately endured in hearing his name so cruelly associated with that of another woman—the woman of whom she had heard from his own lips that she had been his first love)—that room alone was witness to the very tempest of grief to which she now gave way.

CHAPTER IV.

MORE CHANGES THAN ONE.

ANY one who, about two months after that evening on which Hammond had called upon Anthony Northover concerning his niece, had walked along the northern high road which led from Blackhampton to Keriden, and which Hammond and Gerald Triptree had once traversed in company, would have been conscious of the existence of abnormally large and newly-posted placards, which, in gigantic letters, heralded the approach of a sale by auction.

On every piece of blank wall, on every space of wooden paling, upon every finger-post, and upon every tree which was large enough to display even a portion of them, these placards had been posted, while every

public-house and every wayside shop displayed one in its windows ; and so large was
the type that even a brisk walker, whose
mind was dwelling upon other things, could
not fail to be aware that on a certain day
there would be offered for sale, " the dining-
room suite in mahogany," " the drawing-room
suite in fine walnut," " the rich velvet pile
and other carpets," " The articles of virtu,"
" the choice collection of modern paintings,"
" the stud of well-known horses," " the carriages," " the harness," " the rich feather beds
and bedding," and finally the " house " itself,
of some individual, who, either voluntarily or
under compulsion, was breaking up a home
which with care and expense had been got
together.

So much a stranger might notice ; but
many a worthy denizen of Blackhampton was
startled when he saw that the words which
were printed in the largest letters of all were
"that well-known and genteel family residence
' The Shrubs,' " and on a further examination
discovered that the immediate cause of the
sale was, " *in re* Thomas Triptree."

For this man, who had so cleverly made

his own fortune, and whose experience might surely have been sufficient to have warned him against wild speculation, had been caught in his own toils, and in the very height of his prosperity had found himself irretrievably ruined.

Tempted by success, and flattered by the name for shrewdness which his achievements in money-making had gained for him, Mr. Triptree had during the last few years of his life greatly enlarged the circle of his dealings, and to no inconsiderable degree had speculated. Occasionally the gaining of large sums of money would tempt him to launch out even yet further; but more frequently he would by unforeseen and heavy losses be urged on, by the desire to recoup himself, until he found himself entirely out of his depth. It is possible that, had he at this time paid the same rigid and self-denying attention to business which he had done in his earlier and most successful days, he would have done well, and have justified his reputation; but he had now learned to lead and to like a life of pleasure, and unless he could devote two or three days a week to hunting, he was as unhappy as he would have been if he had been deprived of his good dinners, his bottle of port, and his whisky and water.

Thus, relying on his "cuteness," he had, before he even knew it, completely involved himself, and, trying to save himself by a succession of bold strokes, which usually suggested themselves to him while he was under the influence of stimulants, insolvency stared him in the face.

Under these conditions it needed but one of those temporary panics which periodically agitate the money market to bring about the pending crash, and the day arrived on which "The Shrubs" had to accommodate a "man in possession."

The appearance of the exterior of "The Shrubs" was in these altered days sadly changed for the worse. Where everything had once been neat and trim, even to a fault, neglect and disorder were gradually making themselves apparent. The gravel carriage-drive, which Mr. Triptree had delighted to see rolled and kept as firm and as smooth as though it had been paved with asphalte, had been cut up by wheels, and so allowed to

remain ; the geometrical flower borders were
untidy, the lawn was unmown, and the iron
gates, which had been kept as rigidly closed
as though they had guarded a convent, were
left open.   But the worst change of all was
the innumerable announcements of the coming
sale which were stuck all over the walls,
covering the neat and excellent brick-work,
and advertising the ruin of the man who had
in all these things taken such interest and
pride.

In his arm-chair by the fireside, brooding
over the fact that neither chair nor hearth
would be much longer his, Mr. Triptree sat
disconsolate.   The sale was to take place in
but a few days' time, and every article of the
substantial furniture, of the goodness and
strength of which he had so delighted to
boast, was disfigured with its catalogued
number, with which, also, the pictures on the
walls and the ornaments on the mantel-piece
were decorated, and which had not even
spared the easy-chair in which, as he had
done for many years, Mr. Triptree now sat,
and which announced itself as " Lot 23."

As he thus sat the door opened, and, with

catalogue in one hand and pencil in the other, Anthony Northover entered the room. A few months ago how boisterous would have been the welcome which Mr. Triptree would have given him, with what eagerness would he have descended into his cellar and produced a bottle of his best wine, and how noisy would have been his hospitality! Now he was painfully conscious of the fact that all his wine was numbered in lots, and no longer belonged to him; and in Anthony he merely saw one who, having come with an authorised " Card to view," had as good a right in the house, and a greater interest in its belongings, than he had himself.

But, as it turned out, Anthony's visit had been prompted by other motives than those of either curiosity or interest.

" Well," he said, seating himself in a chair opposite to Mr. Triptree, " I've been round, and I can see there'll be a fine sale."

" There ought to be," said Mr. Triptree, gloomily. " There ought to be, for there isn't a thing in the place that isn't good and that wasn't bought well. But what's that to me now? I'm a bankrupt, and it don't signify to

me whether ten or twelve shillings in the
pound is paid."

"Nonsense," said Anthony; "it matters
to you a great deal. Why, my dear sir, I've
been through the same thing myself, and
though only three and sixpence in the pound
was realised, I can assure you I took a posi-
tive pride in thinking that the extra sixpence
was made by my making the best of things."

"There'll be more than three and sixpence
by a long way, in my case," said Mr. Triptree;
"but I shall be as much cursed by my creditors as you were by yours."

"Oh, but creditors always do curse," said
Anthony. "I caught myself doing it the
other day. But if you'd try and help 'em to
get as much as you can, you'd find it would
ease your mind wonderful."

"I havn't the pluck left to see after things,"
said Mr. Triptree. "I know that everything
is going to be taken from me, and what does
it matter to me what it fetches, or where it
goes to? Have some of this?—it's all I've
got left to offer?"

"Yes, I'll have a drop," said Anthony,
taking the bottle of cheap, advertised, whiskey,

which was pushed towards him, and from which the luckless Mr. Triptree had just helped himself. " I'll have a drop ; but, if you'll excuse plain speaking, I'd be sorry to take as much of it as you do !"

" It's the¬only thing as puts any life into me," said Mr. Triptree, peevishly ; " and you don't make allowances, Northover, for what I've gone through. It was bad enough to put up with the disgrace of Gerald's infernal folly, and his being sold up ; and then for me to follow so soon—it's crushed me, that's what it's done !"

" You're wrong about the lad," said North-over.

" In what way ?"

" Why, instead of being angry with him, you ought to feel sorry for him, for it was his very desire to do something for himself which led him wrong, and not because he wanted to be a drag on others. It wasn't his fault that he fell into the hands of a sharper ; for that man who made the screws for him *was* a sharper ; and I tell you you ought to be sorry for him."

" Sorry for him !" cried Mr. Triptree, in a

rage. "No, damn him, he's made his own bed, let him lie on it. I gave that lad, North-over, as good a chance as father ever yet gave son. I educated him in first-class style; I kept him like a gentleman. I gave him a good house and furnished it for him, and the only wrong thing I ever did by him was letting him marry the girl he wanted to marry : and, after all that, he goes and ruins himself, just at a time when I was half ruined myself, by ordering a thousand infernal cork-screws. I could have forgiven him a lot sooner if he'd ordered a thousand dozen of wine—damn me, if I couldn't !"

"I'll grant you it's annoying," said An-thony ; " but if you'd seen and heard as much about it as I did, I'm certain you'd be more sorry for him than angry with him. The poor lad was crazed over this blessed absurd corkscrew of his ; and even after he'd got his house full of them, thought he was going to make a fortune out of them ; and I know for a fact that he was more anxious to make money so that he might relieve you, than for anything else. I'm told it was the saddest sight in the world to see the poor chap going

round with the samples of the screws, expecting to have any amount ordered, and only
getting laughed at. The very first person he
showed them to was me, and knowing how
deep he'd gone into it, I hadn't the heart to
tell him that I was certain they were no good,
but I praised them up, and insisted on being
allowed to buy one ; and that was the first
and the last he ever sold! About a month
after that I was in London, and was looking
in at the window of an ironmonger's shop,
when I saw him inside showing them. You
never saw such a change in a fellow in your
life. His cheeks were sunk, his eyes were
bright and staring, and his poor hands trem-
bled so that he could hardly show them how
the screw worked ; and when he'd explained
it, in a nervous, bungling way, it was awful to
see how anxious he looked while he waited to
see what they would say of it, and if they
would buy any. There was a little crowd of
shopmen round him, and they passed it from
one to the other, and began grinning and
chaffing him about it ; and one said, he ought
to carry a bottle or two of wine about with
him, so that they could test it properly ; and

Gerald took it seriously, and said, quite
simply, that he would if he could afford it ;
and then they chaffed him more, and when at
last he came out of the shop, without an order,
there were tears in the lad's eyes. He brushed
right up against me without seeing who it
was, so I says, 'What, Gerald, well met, my
lad ! Come and have a glass with an old
friend !' And so we went into a place that
was handy, and Gerald put his little leather
case, which held his samples, and which he'd
taken a pride in having made as smart and as
natty as could be, on the bar, and we sat
down together ; and then I saw how worn
and ill, and shabby, he was.

"'Well, and what luck my boy ?' I said.

"'Not much at present,' he says, with a
sickly looking smile ; ' but I must be patient,
somebody will take it up soon, I'm certain.'

"There was a dish of biscuits on the bar,
and when what I'd ordered to drink was
served, he asks me, going very red, whether
I minded his having one? and when he'd got
one, I knew that I was looking at a hungry
man. Well, then I persuaded him to give up
work for an hour or two and to come and dine

with me ; and after dinner I got everything
out of him. He'd been walking about London
for a fortnight, showing his corkscrews to
every one who would look at them, but selling
devil a one of them, till his pluck was nearly as
much worn out as the soles of his boots ; all
his money was gone, and he hardly dared to
go home, for one of the bills was coming due,
and he knew he couldn't meet it. Well, I
needn't tell you he didn't tell me all this
without breaking down a good bit, and then
I gave him my advice, which was to acknowledge to himself that his corkscrew was a
failure, and to lay all his troubles before you,
for of course I didn't know then that you
were in Queer Street yourself. But it was
touching to see the way in which he held on
to his invention, which he didn't seem as
though he could give up, and he said he must
go on trying for a bit longer, and so he had
three more days at it, and then he gave it up
simply because he hadn't strength left to walk
about any longer. And then I suppose he
did tell you his troubles ?"

" Yes," said Mr. Triptree, " he wrote and
told me what his cursed folly had brought him

to ; and then the bill fell due, and was dis-
honoured, and that confounded sweep who
made the corkscrews for him came to me
about it, expecting, of course, that I should
take it up.   It so happened then that even if
I'd wanted to I couldn't, so I simply d——d
his impudence, and he went about his business, and I can assure you, Northover, that
the only satisfaction I've had in my own losses
is the thought that that scamp has, after all,
got bitten, for he only made them for Gerald
on the strength of my name !"

"And if you'd had no losses yourself,
you'd have paid for them ?" said Anthony.

"No, I shouldn't," said Mr. Triptree,
shortly.   " I should have done just as I have
done.   I gave Gerald every chance in the
world.   He's made his own bed : let him lie
on it !"

"You'd never have seen him sold up, if
you could have helped it ?" said Anthony.

"I would—I swear I would," persisted
Mr. Triptree; "and so I told him when I
last saw him.   I've done with him, Northover.   He and I, and his conceited, stuck-up
wife, have all done with each other.   I should

have liked to have seen that young madam's face the day they were sold up."

" No, you wouldn't," said Anthony. " I saw it, and it wasn't an amusing sight I can tell you. Neither was the sale; although I never heard such roars of laughter in my life, as when the corkscrews were put up in one lot at the end of it, and bought for the price of old metal."

" Where did Gerald and his wife go to ?" asked Mr. Triptree.

" That can't signify to you much, since you've done with them," said Anthony. " If you ask me where they ought to have gone to, I should say they ought to have been invited here; but, if you want to know, they came and stayed along with me."

" You're a good-hearted man, Northover ! And are they staying with you now ?"

" No ; they're not. They've taken lodgings for themselves."

" And who pays for them ?"

" Gerald does. He has taken a clerk's situation."

" Who with ?"

" With me ; and a first-rate clerk he is.

He'll get on all right, my friend; you mark that."

" I'm glad to hear it, for I can never do anything for him again."

" And wouldn't if you could."

To this Mr. Triptree made no reply; and, taking this as a sign that he was softening, Anthony said :

" Should you mind seeing Gerald ?"

" I don't want to see him ; but he can come if he likes; and provided he doesn't bring his wife."

" Ah, I forgot;" said Anthony. " That's the only good that has come out of his misfortunes. They've changed his wife. You remember what she was—an unpleasant girl as ever lived ? Well, when Gerald was almost broken-hearted with disappointment, and too ill to do anything, she changed all of a sudden, and became as loving and as active a little woman as you'd wish to see; and that made Gerald another man sooner than anything else. And stay, again—what a forgetful chap I am—I've got a letter here from her to you ! Here it is ! Will you read it ? Perhaps there's an answer to it which I can take back."

It was a nice letter—a far nicer one than those who had known Kate in her earlier days would have thought her capable of writing. In it she commenced by asking Mr. Triptree's pardon for all the foolish airs she had once given herself, and for the want of gratitude for what he had done for her which she had then shown. She touched lightly on their recent troubles, and spoke cheerfully of their present life and future prospects, and begged most earnestly that when Mr. and Mrs. Triptree left "The Shrubs," they would come to their lodgings, where they had already engaged an extra room for them.

And when Mr. Triptree had read this letter, Anthony Northover saw that he was so very much softened that he went straight to Gerald's rooms to tell him so.

The sad story of the disastrous failure of the "Patent Archimedian Self-Acting Corkscrew," and the consequent ruin of its unfortunate proprietor, need not be enlarged upon. Gerald's case was by no means an uncommon one, and so long as there are in the world unprincipled men who will flatter an inventor

on that which is naturally his weakest
point—to wit, his invention—many a poor
fellow, being himself blind to the imperfec-
tions and infatuated with what he deems the
perfections of the production of his brain and
his hands, will sacrifice his money and his
health in vain endeavours to make the public
think as he thinks, and for his pains get
nothing but the laughter and derision of the
indifferent, and the contemptuous pity of
those who understand his unhappy case.

Anthony Northover had succinctly told the
story to the indignant Mr. Triptree, though
he had omitted to add that in his kindly help,
given just at the right moment, Gerald had
found his salvation.   Anthony was a man
who had had monetary troubles of his own,
and now that he was prosperous, although he
was still on some points hardly so punctilious
as he might have been, he delighted to
practise that virtue which covers a multitude
of sins, and so he had taken into his own
house the young couple who were so suddenly
deprived of their own home; had given
Gerald a clerkship in his office, at a salary
which would at least keep him, his wife, and

child in the ordinary necessities of life; and finding that his kindness was not thrown away, held out hopes of still further helping them.

The lodgings which under these circumstances Gerald had taken, and in which they were now living, were, as a matter of necessity, of the plainest and cheapest order, but notwithstanding this they were, as will shortly be seen, likely to prove to him a much happier home than in his married life he had yet known.

When Anthony Northover, fresh from his interview with Mr. Triptree, presented himself in the meagrely furnished room which did the usual duties of a sitting-room, and not unfrequently those of a kitchen, he was the witness of an impoverished but not unpleasant scene. It was about an hour past midday, and Gerald was expected home to his dinner, for which Kate was now presumably preparing: the plain deal table was already spread with a coarse, but clean cloth, on which half a loaf of bread, and a salt-cellar, bore each other company, and Kate herself, wearing a large white apron, and with her sleeves carefully tucked up over the round white arms which she had been wont to protect so religiously from anything which might be likely to produce the damaging evidence of derogatory household work, was on her knees before the fire, anxiously contemplating the frizzling of some slices of bacon, and the boiling of a saucepanful of potatoes.

Could this be Kate, who had been prone to recline on couches, to trifle with fancy work, and to deprecate any sort of occupation which would have been liable to have soiled her dainty little fingers ? Could that subdued, but cheerful face which, when it turned and saw Anthony, wore a bright welcoming smile, be the face of the young lady who had been wont to see everything through a cloud of discontent, and which in the trivial disappoint-ments of her early married life, had threatened to become indelibly stamped with an expression of peevishness, which would for ever have spoiled its otherwise acknowledged beauty ?

Yes, this was Kate, who when she saw her loving husband, who to gratify a wish of hers, would have made any personal sacrifice, who

had ever in his devotion to her been little
short of servile, who had for himself never
expressed a desire or uttered a complaint—
when she saw him utterly cast down, well-
nigh heart-broken at [the failure of that at
which he had so patiently toiled, and almost
helpless in mind and in body, had allowed
her whole system to undergo a complete
change, and after one great flood of tears for
her want of appreciation of the love which
had been lavished on her, resolved to try to
deserve it in the future.

" Well!" said Kate, jumping up and eagerly
addressing Anthony. " Have you seen him ?
and will he come ?"

" I have seen him," said Anthony, " and
I think he'll come; but he's a tough old
file, my dear, and takes his own time to
melt."

" I am so grateful to you," said Kate, " for
taking this matter in hand for me. You may
smile at my saying so so soon after our misfortunes, but if Mr. and Mrs. Triptree come
to us, and I can feel that Gerald and I are
really doing something for them, I shall be
truly happy !"

"H'm," said Anthony somewhat dubiously. " And what does Gerald say about it ?"

" Oh, Gerald does not know, and it will be his surprise that will make me happy. Do you wonder, Mr. Northover, why I am so anxious Mr. and Mrs. Triptree should come to us ?"

" Well, since you ask me, I do, rather. For you see, whatever allowances you may make for his own troubles, he hasn't been as amiable since the corkscrew business as he might have been."

" I will tell you," said Kate blushing prettily. " Gerald never spoke sternly to me except on one subject, and that was when I spoke slightingly of his father. He always declared that he was a good father, and that he owed everything to him, and I never would acknowledge it. Gerald is terribly unhappy now because of this estrangement from his father, especially as he too is in such trouble, but though he has written once or twice, his letters are returned unopened. Now, Mr. Northover" (here Kate turned away and, while she continued talking, busied herself with the bacon and potatoes), " I

know I am right in saying, that in most
ways Gerald is happier now than he has been
for a long time, and I want him to be quite
happy in all ways ; and if I can be the means
of bringing his father to him again, I shall
be very very thankful."

"And you're a good little wife, my dear !"
cried Anthony enthusiastically, "and I'm
hanged if I'm not glad that——"

The arrival of Gerald, however, interrupted
him and with a glance of understanding at
Kate, he began to talk of other things.

"Well, Mr. Head-clerk," said he, "and
how does the shop go on while I spend my
time in flirting with pretty Mrs. Head-
clerk ?"

Gerald looked somewhat older and more
worn than he did prior to the "Patent
Archimedian Corkscrew" experience, and his
face wore an anxious expression which the
happy look that flitted across it when he
kissed his wife, did not altogether oblite-
rate, but he answered Anthony cheerfully
enough.

"Well, sir," he said, "except that we
missed your genial presence, everything went

on just as though you had been with us, and since our loss has been my wife's gain, I should be the last to complain of your absence."

"Very pretty, indeed," said Anthony. "Mrs. Head-clerk, might I ask whether you would object to become Mrs. Traveller; for upon my word, if this young man can turn out that sort of thing as a regular article I shall be obliged to put him on the road?"

"I should object to it very much indeed," said Kate, "so I shall try and make him cultivate bearishness. But is anything the matter, Gerald? You look as though you had something to tell?"

"Yes," said Gerald. "I have something to tell, and I am glad to meet Mr. Northover here, for though it has shocked and surprised me, it more nearly affects him."

"What is it?" asked Anthony nervously, and turning pale; for he was ever apprehensive of events which might interfere with the even current of his present life of easy-going happiness.

"News has come of the death of Mr. Percy Rockcliffe."

" Whew !" whistled Anthony while the colour returned to his face. " Well, if it's a fact, the world's rid—but there, we won't say anything against the dead, if dead, indeed, he is. How did you hear it ?"

" Kate's sister, Minnie, told me this morning. A letter came to Mr. Hammond Rockcliffe from his relatives at Keriden, saying that the news of his death had come from New York, and requesting that he would tell his widow."

" Well, better widow than wife, say I !" observed Anthony ; "and your friend Mr. Hammond Rockcliffe will now be able to do as he ought by her."

" Mr. Northover !" cried Kate hotly, "you put a very wrong construction upon that matter, and you will live to be sorry for it. Why the simple fact that my sister lives with the poor girl ought to be sufficient to prove to you——"

" Hoighty, toighty my dear !" interrupted Anthony, " don't let us fall out about it! Look here, here's you and the bacon and the potatoes all boiling over at once, and if I don't immediately make myself scarce, I shall spoil a good temper and a good dinner!"

And without waiting for any reply he hurried off.

"I can't help being angry," said Kate, when she was alone with her husband, "whenever anything is said about the abominable scandal which was talked concerning poor Mrs. Percy Rockcliffe and her husband's cousin."

"You can't wonder," said Gerald, "that her conduct, poor creature, gave rise to scandal. For her I have the sincerest compassion, but he was certainly very much to blame in the matter."

"He was thoughtless," said Kate; "but no one shall ever make me believe——"

"*Honi soit qui mal y pense*, my dear wife," said Gerald, interrupting her. "Let us sit down to the bacon and potatoes."

But Kate was not so willing to terminate the subject, and as soon as Gerald had commenced his dinner, she reintroduced it.

"I always thought, Gerald, that you had the very highest opinion of Hammond Rockcliffe?"

"So I had," was the reply.

"And now ?"

"I do not know what to think. I cannot think the evil of him which most people do, and yet he must have known how, by acting towards her as he did, he compromised that poor girl. And then his negligence as her trustee was, to say the least of it, culpable."

"People say, do they not, that the whole thing was a conspiracy between him and his cousin ?"

"Yes ; they do. But I cannot believe it."

"And what do they say of her ?"

"Oh, every one thinks she was a victim !"

"Then every one pities her ? Why then is the poor girl slighted ?"

"Because—the subject is a very painful one to me, and I would rather not pursue it, Kate—because it is said that in some respects she was a willing victim."

"And why is the subject such a painful one to you ?"

"Because I owe him money, and do not know how to pay it !"

"Oh, how like a man's reason that is ! Mine is a woman's reason, but it is one that makes the subject ten times more painful. It is because of poor Minnie."

"It is impossible to legislate for Minnie; she is too self-willed and headstrong. Of course she ought never to have gone to live with her."

"I do not mean because of that," said Kate, somewhat warmly; "that is proof to me of poor Gertrude Rockcliffe's innocence."

"What do you mean then?"

"Did you not once think that Hammond Rockcliffe cared for Minnie?"

"I did; I felt certain of it, and that made me all the more indignant with him. Oh, I hope poor Minnie never cared for him! What do you think, Kate?"

"I do not know; I hope not, for he is sure now to marry his cousin's widow, who, if report speaks truly, was his first love."

"Yes," said Gerald, "I believe that that was so. It is a bad business, and one which it will be difficult to set right; if I were not so unhappy about my own affairs, I should think more of it."

"But you know we agreed to think that

your own affairs were in an exceedingly prosperous condition !"

"And so in some ways, and thanks to you,
dearest Kate, they are ; and when I say that
I have never felt more thankful or happy
than I have done during the last few weeks,
I speak the truth.   I am more troubled about
my poor father's affairs than about my own."

" But his misfortunes are not of your
making ?"

" No ; they are not.   But his misfortunes
should be my misfortunes, and he will not let
me share in them.   I cannot forget, Kate,
how good a father he has been to me, and I
cannot forget that my duty as his son is to
help him in his time of trouble ; and he will
not let me do the little that I am able.   Oh,
Kate, he was such a kind father !"

" I think that he was a mixture ; he blew
hot and cold.   Sometimes he was too indulgent, sometimes too strict."

"Perhaps if he had been less indulgent
and more strict, it would have been better for
me."

" As concerning your marriage, for in-
stance ?"

Gerald rose and coming to his wife kissed her, and said :

" I believe it is because I feel that to him I chiefly owe the great, great happiness of having you for my wife, that I am so anxious to be a good son to him. See here, dearest Kate. His ruin must in any case have been my ruin, but owing to my own execrable folly, my ruin preceded his ; and what was the lesson which it taught me ? that I had the most generous, the most patient, and the most loving wife that the world ever saw. Can you wonder that I want to help the father who helped me to marry such a wife ?"

" All that is nonsense, Gerald ; but you are right to stand by him. You must wait a little, and he will give way."

" I hope so," said Gerald ; " but he is an obstinate man, and one difficult to move."

And again kissing his wife, he betook himself to his work.

But Kate, when she was left to herself, and after she had satisfied the manifold requirements of a most exacting baby, and so set at rest the mind of one whom she firmly believed to be the most intelligent young mother who had ever been blessed with an extraordinarily beautiful infant, allowed her thoughts to revert from the misfortunes of Mr. Triptree and her sincere desire to help her husband in his efforts to assist him, to the affairs of her sister Minnie.

Having for some time dwelt on these she determined that she would without delay see and have a talk with her, and having calculated the hours, and made arrangements for the well-being of the aforesaid babe, she sallied forth to meet Minnie as she returned from her work.

It is pleasant to record that the sisters, when they met, greeted each other far more affectionately than of yore they would have done.

" Well, Minnie," said Kate, as they turned and walked together, " this is sad news !"

" Yes," said Minnie ; " but when you have read through the first four acts of a domestic tragedy, you are not surprised that there should be a death in the fifth, and we must hope that now the curtain has come down, there are happier days in store for that poor girl."

"How does she bear it; as well as you can expect, I suppose?"

"No; a great deal worse than one has any right to expect. I'm certain that if I were in her place, and had been treated as by that abominable man she has been treated, I should be rejoiced to hear that his wicked life had come to an end, and that I was a free woman. Instead of that she chooses to be plunged in the deepest grief, and is quite a pathetic young widow. She doesn't, you must understand, go off into hysterical lamentations or anything of that sort; she goes about quietly like she always does, and never ceases to try and be pleasant; but you can see by her face that she's suffering, and suffering for that wretch of a man."

"Well that shows she has a good heart," said Kate, "and it also proves how wickedly false that scandal was concerning her and Mr. Rockcliffe."

"I never needed any proof of that," said Minnie. "Well, they'll be able to silence the scandal-mongers now."

"In what way do you mean?"

"Oh, I should think that he would be certain to marry her."

"But you have just said what grief she was in."

"I don't mean that he'll marry her straight away off at once. For decency's sake a certain amount of time must be allowed to elapse, and during that her grief will have an opportunity of subsiding. She's not going to die of sorrow any more than any one else has ever done."

"Do you then think that he cares for her in that way?"

"I know that he *did*, and probably he does, or now that he can think of her in that way very soon will do."

"And what of her?"

"If he asks her, she'll marry him. She's different to me, Kate, and could never get on in the world alone. She must have something to cling to, and, after a manner, she already begins to cling to him. It only requires a very little tact from outside people to bring them together."

"But I don't think, Minnie, that it is any-one's business to do that, nor can I see why the marriage is so much to be desired."

"But I can. You see their position

towards each other is a very peculiar one. In the mysterious absence and silence of her father—a mystery which, I think, can only be accounted for in the supposition that he is dead—she has literally no one in the world to help her except Mr. Rockcliffe. She fancies, poor soul, that a small sum of money out of her squandered fortune was saved for her, and periodically he brings her instalments of it; but it doesn't take a very shrewd person to see that it is really he who provides for her this money, so that, in short, he is absolutely supporting her; and when one remembers how her father made him her trustee, and that if he had not been so negligent and careless her money would not have been dissipated, it certainly seems right that he should do so; but whether it is right or wrong, any one who knows him as well as I do, must see that he will keep on doing it to the end of the chapter. Well, when a man and a woman are in this position towards each other, when their names have been as unpleasantly associated together as theirs have been, when it is evident that each is suited to the other, and they would certainly be happy as husband and wife, does it not seem that the best and the wisest thing that they can do would be to be married ?"

" Oh, I· quite see the force of your arguments," said Kate; " but other questions arise, one of which is, is he free to marry, or is there not some one else who would make him an equally good wife, and who has an equal claim upon him ?"

" I think not," said Minnie decidedly.

" Minnie," said Kate, " do you mind my asking you a plain question ?"

Minnie did mind very much, for she foresaw what was coming; but, feeling there was for her no alternative, she said :

" Not at all. What do you want to know ?"

" Did you never care for Mr. Rockcliffe ?"

"Oh, I always liked him very much indeed."

" That is no answer. At one time it was apparent to every one that he was paying you very marked attention, and it was equally apparent that you did not discourage him. Was it not so ?"

" You said so," said Minnie, with a curious little laugh, in which there was more of scorn

than of amusement, although she meant that
it should convey the sense of the latter—
" you said so, Kate, and called me over the
coals about it, and seeing that everything
which you said was wise and true, of course
I never allowed myself to think of him except
in the light of a friend."

Kate coloured deeply, and said :

"Things have changed with me since that
time, Minnie, and I trust that I have changed
with them. Oh, I do hope that you did not
think seriously of anything which I then said.
If I thought that I had in any way brought a
cloud on the happiness of your life, I could
never forgive myself or enjoy any happiness
again."

" Reassure yourself, my dear sister," said
Minnie. "If you'll think for one instant
you'll remember that I never took any one's
advice in my life, but always judged and
acted for myself."

" Then you never did, and do not, love Mr.
Rockcliffe ?"

" That is the exact state of the case," said
Minnie, fervently trusting that this offence
against the truth was one which the record-

ing angel, understanding her motives, would graciously condone.

"You have taken quite a load off my mind," said Kate. " Directly I heard of his cousin's death it seemed such a natural thing to think that he would marry the widow, and then, dear Minnie, I thought so anxiously of you, and of what you might feel. Now that you have confided in me I do not mind, and I think that the sooner they are married the better; and if there is only to be found a man good enough I should say the same thing of you, though if, you naughty girl, you flirt as openly as I now see you did with Mr. Rockcliffe, I'm afraid you'll find a difficulty in it. Why, every one thought you were in love with him, Minnie!"

" But I was always a problem to every one. Here we are at home; will you come in and see Gertrude? I wish you would; it will cheer her up."

Minnie's rooms, poor as they were in their appointments, were as neat and orderly as Minnie herself; and in them Gertrude, whose pretty figure was clothed in a very simple black dress, but who, except for this, was undisfigured by what are known as "widow's weeds," formed a not unpleasing picture.

The grateful and contented smile which, when she looked up and saw Minnie, lit up her sorrow-stricken face, showed plainly that Gertrude had made a dear and true friend, and one in whom she implicitly trusted. There was very much of the protectress, too, in the air with which Minnie affectionately kissed her; and near of an age as the two young girls were, it could at a glance be seen which was the one who in all things relied upon the other.

When Kate said to her a few words of tender sympathy, the tears coursed down poor Gertrude's cheeks; but it was evident that, though she was suffering, she was making great efforts to avoid all outward signs of great grief, and afterwards she was able to speak quite quietly of other things, until Kate, with her mind greatly relieved as regards Minnie, hurried off to her precious baby.

Minnie and Gertrude had now lived together sufficiently long not only to feel perfectly at home in each other's company, but also to have established a firm and, what promised to be, a lasting friendship. From the night on which Hammond Rockcliffe had brought her to her present lodgings, Gertrude had felt that in Minnie she had found a protectress, and that which she so sorely needed —a friend of her own age and sex, who could sympathise with her, and in whom she could confide ; and as she had a thousand simple but pretty ways of her own, in which she evinced her pleasure at this acquisition, and her gratitude for every little act of tenderness and kindness which was shown her, Minnie, in spite of herself, could not help being drawn towards her, and very soon became unfeignedly attached to her.

Those words, *"in spite of herself,"* must be written, because it must be confessed that Minnie, notwithstanding that her offer to assist the poor friendless girl had been a purely voluntary one, could not help recognising in her a dangerous rival for Hammond's affections. Was she not, on his own telling, the first woman whom he had ever loved, and was it not as true as truth can be that, however strong a second love may be, the memory

of a first, even after a lapse of years, is dan-
gerously intense? And had not this recent
· abominable scandal, discard it as she would,
been to her so painful that it had shown her
more clearly than anything else had done how
deep her own love for Hammond was? Had
it not been terrible to her to think that, however innocent his attachment might be, he
should take so much interest in this girl that
he had taken her under his own roof, and
had, when all her other friends had deserted
her, there tended her?

Thus, though Minnie had received Gertrude
with a firm resolve that all that her creed
taught her that one woman should do for
another she would do, it was only natural
that she should, from one point of view (and
that one the nearest of anything to her own
heart), regard her with suspicion; and it
speaks well for Gertrude's powers of making
herself beloved that she was so soon able to
forget this in a new and a sincere affection.

Their life together was a quiet and simple
one. Minnie was again applying herself assi-
duously to her old work at Northover and
Weskut's in the workshop at Triptree's mill,

and Gertrude, anxious to be occupied, and
desirous of eking out her limited means, had,
through the agency of Hammond Rockcliffe,
met with some employment in the way of
fancy needlework, for which she received
modest emolument. The poor young creature
was delighted to think that she could earn
money ; and it was lucky for her that at this
time she never visited Hammond's rooms, for
had she done so, and had she seen there
all her handiwork in Berlin wools, cords,
beads, braids, and cottons, lying as so much
"dead stock," and could she have imagined
the efforts which at times it cost her patron
to find the money wherewith to pay for them,
the credit which she was disposed to bestow
upon herself would have been rudely dis-
persed.

As a matter of course, Hammond came
constantly to visit the two young girls ; for,
feeling that he was in every way responsible
for Gertrude's welfare, he was hardly satisfied
to let a day go by without seeing her, and,
notwithstanding his anxiety concerning her
future, and his personal misgivings respecting
her past, it is possible that he found no small

amount of pleasure in their companionship
and society.

To Minnie his visits were at first exceedingly painful.   With all her strength she was
endeavouring to wean herself from her love
for him, and to forget the dream of happiness
in which she had once indulged; for from the
day on which she had made up her mind that
she would not be a suitable wife for him, and
that a marriage with her would retard his
progress in life and mar his position in society,
she had never for a single moment suffered
herself to swerve from the resolution which
she had then formed; but though in his absence she was able to be brave about her
trouble, she found that his constant presence
was to her a source of great distress, and that
at times the reopening of old wounds, to which
she was thus subjected, was almost more than
she could endure.

It was, too, perhaps a little bit aggravating
to her to see how completely Hammond had
taken her at her word, and how little likely
he seemed to be to renew his protestations.
It seemed strange to her that he should be
able to visit and converse with her as though

nothing like love-making had ever passed between them ; and though she told herself that she ought to be grateful to him, she could not help a feeling of annoyance, which was all the more painful to her inasmuch as she had to acknowledge to herself how inconsistent and absurd her annoyance was.

The explanation of Hammond's conduct is that he had thoroughly made up his mind that he must give up all thought of gaining a woman's affection, or of attaining happiness by marriage. He still loved Minnie, and to have won her love in return he would willingly have laid down his life ; but he told himself that it was impossible that she could ever love him, and that the right as well as the wisest thing to do, was to accept the answer which she had given him as final, and as much as he could, therefore, he strove to banish her from his thoughts. He felt, too, that the circumstances which had again brought them together were in all ways untoward, but his dilemma concerning Gertrude had been so great, and Minnie's generous offer had been so opportune, that he did not feel himself to be in a position to consult his own feelings in the matter.

But as time went on, and they became used to seeing each other frequently, these sentiments in both of them wore away, and at the time of the intelligence of Percy Rockcliffe's death, there was between them little or no constraint.

Now it was Minnie's nature to take in view one object, and for the attainment of her desires concerning it, to overcome all obstacles, and to set at nought all difficulties, and at any personal trouble or sacrifice to gain her end.

At the present time the chief object of her life was to make Gertrude happy. She had taken her under her protection, and she had learnt to love her; and she felt that her work would be badly and but half done if she did not finally and happily re-establish her in a home of her own.

It is not surprising that Percy's death immediately suggested to her the possibility of Hammond marrying his first love; and though, at first, this end to her own chances of happiness seemed too horrible to be entertained, reflection told her how appropriate, on all accounts, such a marriage would be, and so she resolved that it should be brought about, and that through her.

"I'm afraid I shall feel rather like my old friend the Spartan boy," she said to herself; " but I must get over that, and I had better resemble him than the ' dog in the manger.' I don't want, or at all events I'm not going to have, Hammond for myself, and why should I deny him to another, who will be happy with him and make him a good wife ? Besides, it will ' clench ' matters for us all—for her, for him, and for me. When you have made up your mind what is best to be done, there is nothing like ' clenching ' things. One can't be shilly-shally when things are well clenched."

And so she set to work to clench them, finding, however, that her task was not one so speedily to be accomplished as she had imagined. Time went on, and Hammond, as usual, came and went, and Gertrude ceased to weep for her dead husband, or, if she wept, it was only when she was alone—and so far all was well ; but except that the friendship between the two became daily stronger and more tender, her reliance upon him more implicit, and her dependence . upon him more complete, neither showed the least sign that any thought that any relation stronger than that of friendship could ever exist between them, had as yet developed itself.

"They must be told of it," said Minnie to herself. "If they can't see what's good for them they must be shown, or they'll go on just as they are now, till they are old and grey-headed, and then perhaps it will one day occur to them both, 'Dear me, why shouldn't we be married?' and then the match, of course, will be an absurd one. There is nothing I dislike more than a marriage between old people."

And so one day this determined young lady said to Hammond, when they chanced to be alone together :

"Mr. Rockcliffe, I wonder when you will think of getting married ? Why do you not do so ?"

For a moment Hammond looked at her in mute astonishment, and when he spoke there was indignation in his voice :

"Why do I not marry ? Of all people, Minnie Tryan, you should be the last to ask me that question, since you know better than any one the answer to it !"

Minnie reddened, and said in a subdued voice :

"Of course I know what you allude to, Mr. Rockcliffe, but I need hardly say that that was not in my mind when I spoke. I hoped that you had forgotten that old nonsense about me."

"It was not nonsense, and I shall never forget it," said Hammond, hotly ; "although you have long ago made me believe that it is best for my own peace of mind that I should try to do so !"

"And that is just what I would have you think," said Minnie, earnestly. "Indeed, it was because I thought that you had long ago arrived at that conclusion, and had reconciled yourself to it, that I spoke to you as I did."

"Must I reconcile myself to it ?" asked Hammond. "God only knows how I have striven to do so, and how hard to me the struggle has been !"

"But it is a struggle of the past now," said Minnie ; "and you are too experienced a doctor to reopen an old wound. Now, may I

repeat my question—why do you not think of
getting married ?"

Again Hammond looked at her in astonishment, and said :

" Do you wonder that, after what has just
passed between us, I am at a loss to imagine
what you are thinking of, or what you
mean ?"

Minnie laughed now, as she said :

" I did not think you would require me to
be so very explicit.   It seemed to me so probable that your mind should have been full of
the same thoughts as filled my own, so natural
that, now things are as they are, you should
think of making Gertrude your wife."

" Gertrude !   My wife !   Good Heavens,
Minnie, what do you mean ?"

" Just what I say.   It seems to me that,
situated as you are towards each other, it
would be the natural as well as the right
thing.   I know, as well as you do, that you
are supporting her, though you keep her in
ignorance of it.   That is all wrong.   Why
should you not support her as your wife?
We know very well that, with the exception
of yourself, she has literally no one to help or

to care for her. You could much better help her and care for her if you were her husband. All the unkind stories which were afloat concerning you, and which, do what you will, must continue to injure you both, would, by your marriage, be silenced; and I firmly believe that by it your happiness would be secured."

" I declare to you, Minnie, that this is the first time that such a thought has ever suggested itself to me !"

" Then take my advice, and encourage it."

" But, Minnie, you know so well why I have not the heart to think of marriage !"

" And I know so well that you have the heart to make such a good husband !"

" Oh, Minnie ! Can you give me no hope ?"

" None," said Minnie, firmly ; " none, as regards myself. I believe, Hammond, that I must be heartless. I should never be able to make you happy, but I should dearly love to see you so ; and I believe that there is happiness for you in that which I have suggested."

And feeling that she had, as it were, " laid the ground," Minnie said no more. Poor girl ! the task had been a harder one than she had anticipate 1, for Hammond's avowed constancy to herself touched her nearly and tempted her sorely; but she was firm of purpose, and, though she had many an inward heartache and many a struggle, she did not swerve from her determination.

On the following evening, and when they were sitting sewing together, she made an attack on Gertrude.

"How true it is that circumstances alter cases," she said. "It seems to me that one never makes up one's mind upon an important subject but some unforeseen occurrence shows us that, under a different light, our opinions are of no use at all."

"I think we all find that out as we grow older," said Gertrude. "Are you thinking specially of any one thing, Minnie ?"

"Yes—I am ; I am thinking of second marriages. I used to abominate the very idea of them, and I well remember saying, when I was a very little girl, that if ever my mother married again I should hate her and would run away from home, and I really believe I should have done so. Indeed, I think that where there are children I

should never, about a second marriage, alter
my mind, but without them the thing is
different. Now, when you are married again,
dear, I shall rejoice."

" When I am married again ?" cried Gertrude, looking up with a flushed, troubled,
and startled face. " Oh, Minnie, what do
you mean ? I shall never marry again."

" About that you will of course please
yourself," said Minnie; " but you had better
not make too strong a resolution, or when
it is brought home to you, as it has been to
me, that circumstances *do* alter cases, you
will feel small."

" I am thankful to think," said Gertrude,
still flushed, and timidly indignant, " that in
my present quiet life I am unlikely to have
any opportunity of marrying again."

" My dear little lady," said Minnie, " then
you must be either very blind or very much
more artful than I ever thought you to be !
I should say if any one ever had an opportunity of marrying again, and of marrying
well too, it is you."

" What *do* you mean, Minnie ?"

" What do I mean, you funny puss ? Why

do you think Mr. Hammond Rockcliffe is so assiduous in his visits here ?"

"Mr. Rockcliffe? Oh, Minnie! You know he is my oldest, my best, and, in short, my only friend."

"And don't you think that your oldest, your best, and your only friend would make you a very good husband? Or that he, regarding you in the same light, thinks that you would make him a very nice little wife? Mind, I know nothing of his feelings in the matter, I only guess; but I think it is only right that I should tell you what he is doing for you."

And in a few words she told the young widow that the periodically paid sums upon which she was subsisting were not, as she imagined, the remnant of her own squandered fortune, but the hard-earned moneys of Hammond Rockcliffe.

When she had finished Gertrude rose, looking sadly scared, and with great tears in her eyes.

"I do not know what to say, Minnie," she said. "You have taken me so much by surprise. I can only pray to God that it is not with him as you seem to believe. I knew that I owed him a life-long gratitude, though never till this moment did I realise the extent to which he is my benefactor. But I can never, never marry again."

And so saying she hurried from the room.

"The correct thing for her to say, but nonsense for all that," said Minnie, left alone and plying her needle after a determined, not to say vicious, fashion. " Well, I have done my best, and if they don't make each other happy it won't be my fault. We shall see what comes of it."

Without taking into account her own and Gertrude's tears, for, for some cause or another, both these young ladies passed some restless and unhappy nights, the immediate result of Minnie's negotiations was, ostensibly, failure of the most direct kind, for between the two whom she wished to bring together there immediately arose an embarrassment and constraint which seemed insurmountable, and which put all their former pleasant inter-course to flight.

But on the whole Minnie was satisfied with the first effects of her experiment. She had not anticipated that the idea of marriage would have been so strange to Hammond and Gertrude as evidently it was, and she knew that both must get used to thinking of it before anything more could be done; and so she resolved to watch patiently the working of her scheme.

But the comfort of the little party had now quite gone, and Hammond's visits instead of being to Gertrude a source of pleasure were as distressing to her as they were to him. Regarding him in this new light she lived in daily expectation that he would ask her a question to which she felt that in common gratitude she could make but one answer; and for reasons of her own the bare thought of this was sufficient to destroy the little that was left to her of the happiness of life, and Hammond was almost overwhelmed by the thoughts which since his conversation with Minnie had filled his mind, for, do what he would, he could not help seeing and acknowledging the sense and the force of her views, or being impressed with the idea that perhaps the most direct way of fulfilling his strange and delicate duties towards Gertrude would be to make her his wife.

To make Gertrude his wife ! Strange that the dream of happiness of a few years ago should wear so different an aspect now !

And so things became daily more uncomfortable, and watchful Minnie predicted to herself that a crisis was at hand.

Minnie was right. Hammond noticed Gertrude's drooping spirits and pale, sad face, and telling himself that the fault might be his, resolved to hesitate no longer.

" Gertrude," he said one evening when they were alone together in her plain sitting-room, " do you ever think of the days when we first knew each other ? Of the time when your poor mother died, and of that which followed ?"

Gertrude anticipated what was coming, and her heart beat quickly as she said :

" Yes ; at times I think a great deal of those days. It is not likely that I should ever forget them."

" You know what I then felt for you ?"

" I do. But I believe it was better as it was. I was not worthy of you."

" Before your mother died I made her a promise that throughout my life I would do my utmost to befriend and to serve you."

"And never has promise been more nobly fulfilled," said Gertrude, taking his hand in hers, and looking at him gratefully.

"Alas, no!" said Hammond bitterly. "But for me and my folly you would not have been as you are now."

"Oh, do not think of that," she said earnestly. "I hoped that you had long ago ceased to think of that. It is I, rather, who should feel remorse that I and my affairs have so embittered your life."

"Do you believe in destiny, Gertrude? It sometimes seems to me as though our destinies must be the same. How strangely, after all that has passed, you and I have been brought together again!"

"Indeed we have. But rather than believe it to be destiny I would think that God has given me in this world one good and loyal friend who never has, for a moment, deserted me."

"Then let that friend be to you all that he once so ardently wished. The years which have gone by, Gertrude, since I once asked you to be my wife have brought much trouble to both of us ; but now, as then, my great object in life is to help and to serve you. Will you be my wife now, Gertrude ?"

Some moments elapsed before she could sufficiently control herself to answer him, and then, with a great effort, she looked up into his face and said :

"Yes, Hammond, I will."

* * * * *

" I wonder," said Gertrude to Minnie a few days later, and when she was able to talk calmly of her new prospects, " I wonder if a woman was ever before blessed with such a steadfast, self-denying love as his has been for me. I have told you how he loved me when I was quite a young girl, and you see he has ever since been constant to me. Surely I ought to do everything in my power to reward such a love as that !"

" Certainly you should," said Minnie. " It falls to the lot of very few women to be the sole object of a man's affection."

CHAPTER V.

'TWIXT CUP AND LIP.

THERE was little need that the engagement between Hammond and Gertrude should be of long duration.   There were no parents who would require their feelings to be consulted, no marriage settlements to be drawn, no wedding guests to be invited, no trousseau to be prepared ; neither had Hammond to await that time when he should be in a " position " to marry, he having made up his mind that, under the circumstances, such position as he was to make for himself and for his wife might be as well attained after marriage as before, and for his bride's home he contented himself with taking pretty and comfortable rooms in a better and more open part of the town than that in which his old ones were situated.

All these things considered, therefore, it seemed to Minnie that when from the day on which matters had been "clenched" two months had elapsed and the wedding day had not been fixed, an unnecessary and absurd delay was taking place, and the anxious little soul became, as she witnessed the apparent disinclination of "her young people," as she called them, to act for themselves, not a little disturbed.

But at length the day, the hour and the place were alike decided upon, and the disinterested girl confidently looked forward to the successful issue of that for which she had striven so hard, and for which she had made so many sacrifices.

It was within a few days of that one on which the two lives, which had been so curiously connected, were to be made as one, that Hammond, after a long and tiring day's work, hailed a cab and ordered himself to be driven, reflecting that it would be almost for the last time, to his old quarters.

The vehicle in which he found himself was

a splendid specimen of a provincial "hansom."
Weak on what were once its "springs," rotten as to its woodwork, cracked as to its
glass, damp, seared, and torn as to its leather,
musty and dusty as to its upholstery, and
horribly suggestive as to the stuffing, which
from the many places in which it was torn
protruded itself from it—the wonder was not
only that people could be found who would
ride in it, but that the structure held together
at all.　To attempt to get any ease or comfort out of it was impossible, for to lean back
in it was to feel that you would never regain
a perpendicular position ; and to lean forward
in it was to run a serious risk of being
guillotined by the rattling, up-folded glass
window, which was supported by a manifestly rotten cord.　The driver, too, had, by a
habit which he had contracted of continually
reversing his position in the seat at the back
from a sitting to a standing one, acquired a
knack of making the whole concern sway and
oscillate to a degree that would have rendered a bad sailor sea-sick.　But worse than
the cab was the poor decrepit quadruped
which was attached to it.　Broken-kneed,

semi-blind, bone-protruding, and in but too
many places raw-skinned; chafed everywhere
by ill-fitting and fast-rotting harness, half-fed,
ill-shod, and un-groomed, this poor quivering
creature yet plodded patiently along in a
manner which might have taught a useful
lesson to many a human being. The only
thing about this abominable conveyance (for
the privilege of riding in which an exorbitant
fare and a round of abuse from a foul-mouthed
driver were invariably exacted) which seemed
in anything like repair or working order was
the cruel thong of gutta-percha attached to
the lash of the long whip, and which, while
doing continual and heavy execution on the
flinching flesh of the horse, occasionally
varied the monotony of the performance by
flicking full into the face of the cab's occupant, thus keeping him in a state of lively
excitement as to the safety of his eye-sight.

More than once did Hammond remonstrate
with the driver on the cruel way in which he
flogged his horse, and the brutal way in which
he growled forth oaths and anathemas, and
fifty times more than once, and whenever a
perfect rain of wicked cuts had induced the

unfortunate animal to relapse from his sham-
bling trot into a wearied and awkward canter,
thus causing him to roll about like a tempest-
tossed mariner, did he regret his folly and
extravagance in not trusting to his own tired
legs rather than to this publicly-licensed conveyance; and when he, at length, got out at the
corner of his own street, he spoke very plainly
to the cabman concerning his treatment of
the poor brute which was entrusted to his
care.

"Lord bless you, sir," said the cabman, as
he pocketed his fare (and something over and
beyond his fare), "that's just the way with
you gents. You don't know this 'ere 'orse as
well as me. It ain't that he can't go, but
that he won't. Why, bless you, he could do
his twenty mile an hour easy if he only chose,
but he's artful, sir, downright artful; that's
what he is. Look at him now, pretending
he's wore out. Now then, artful!"

Thus accosted, and feeling a tug at the
rein, which well-nigh forced part of an ill-
shaped bit into the soft flesh of his mouth,
this knowing animal, who had certainly been
giving a marvellously clever portraiture of

fatigue, roused himself, and was about to resume his labours, when a sudden uproar rivetted the attention not only of Hammond, but of the cabman, and gave him a few moments' respite.

They had stopped at the foot of a hill and at the junction of several streets ; one of these, it was that from which the noise proceeded, presented another steep hill, and down this, at lightning speed, came a spectacle which made the blood run cold.

A cab horse of very different calibre to the cunning quadruped of Hammond's recent acquaintance, an animal which had probably been sold for his vice, and which possibly was having its first experience of work between the shafts, had taken the law into his own hands and the bit between his teeth, and *ventre-à-terre* was galloping down the declivity, bringing along with him, as though it had been the weight of a feather, the cab to which he was harnessed, and which bounded and rocked from side to side in a manner terrible to witness,—while the pale scared faces of the helpless driver and still more helpless occupant, were dreadful to a degree.

A moment before and the street had been well-nigh empty and deserted. Now, and as if by magic, it became a perfect sea of excited human beings, who starting forth on all sides, closed up in a crowd behind the runaway cab, and at the best pace at their command, followed to see its doom; from every window and from every doorway eager faces were stretched out, and with one accord this suddenly conjured-up multitude did the very worst thing which could be done, and shouting and bawling, "Stop him!"."Stop him!" maddened to ten degrees more the already-frenzied horse.

Down the hill they came, and nearer and nearer to Hammond approached those horrible, frightened faces, which saw nothing before them but a violent and ghastly death. "How is it to end?" he thought, and sickened as he thought it. "Is it possible that they can keep clear of everything, or will they be dashed into atoms?"

Denser and louder grew the crowd, and still more rapid became the pace of the runaway horse, who galloped as he had never galloped before. To attempt to stop him would have been certain death, and Hammond could only hope that having completed the descent of the one hill in safety, the ascent of the other would serve to arrest the frantic progress, when just as they came close to them the artful cab-horse, who had again put on a simulated appearance of weariness, being possibly infused with an idea that an unforeseen opportunity of putting an end to a joyless existence was offered to him, settled the matter by calmly turning round and placing himself and his cab directly across the roadway.

There was one loud cry of agony, a great crash of broken glass and woodwork, a terrific plunging of horses, and a wild on-pressing of the seething, yelling crowd.

" He's down !" " He's up again ;" " They're both killed !" " No, only one !" " Sit on his head !" " Cut his traces !" " Pull the cab off them !" "Yah !" "He's off again !" " No, by G—d, he's stopped !" " Well done, young man !" " Well done !" " Hooray !"

Such were the disjointed sentences in which these frantic and useful members of the British public indulged, the last ones having special reference to Hammond, who, watching his opportunity, rushed at the runaway horse when he was down, and seizing him with experienced hands, proved to the half-stunned, bewildered brute that though all the strength might be on his side, he had met his master.

A dozen hands were now ready to assist him, and bleeding from many cuts, and steaming and panting from fright and exhaustion, the wretched animal was unfastened from what had been the cab, and led on one side.

Hammond now pressed forward to look after the human beings, for whose fate he had the worst apprehensions. It was a gruesome sight. From beneath the ruin of the two cabs, and the carcass of the artful one, who had received the jagged end of a broken shaft in his vitals and had ceased to exist, they had already lifted one inanimate body —that of the driver; and a score pair of hands were lifting the heavy *débris* for the rescue of the second.

On all sides there were loud cries for a doctor.

" Permit me," said Hammond, pressing forward, " I am a doctor."

The crowd gave way for him, and he was the first to see the bleeding face of the maimed and apparently lifeless man.

" Yah !" roared those nearest to Hammond, and who saw a great and sudden change come over him, " Him call himself a doctor, and can't face the sight of blood ! Yah !"

But it was the sight of the man rather than of his wounds which caused Hammond such extreme agitation that he felt everything about him to be moving in a giddy whirl so that he could hardly stand. For a moment he felt utterly powerless, but immediately summoning together all his resources, he partially recovered his presence of mind, and, kneeling beside the body, carefully examined the pallid features to convince himself, that in that wild, terrible thought which had shot through his brain, there was no truth.

But he only did so to find his extraordinary suspicion verified. The body was worn and wasted with want and disease, the clothes were misfitting and shabby to a degree ; but the face, disfigured as it was with bleeding gashes, was none the less the face of the man whom they had all believed to be dead—the face of his cousin, Percy Rockcliffe!

Some preparations had now been made by the crowd to convey the sufferers to the nearest hospital, and three men stepped forward to raise the lifeless form.

" I know this man," said Hammond ; " let him be brought to my lodgings, which are close at hand."

And so there they brought him, and, laying him upon the bed—it was the same one which Gertrude had so recently occupied—left the two alone together.

For a short time Hammond was so completely stupefied that he was wholly unequal to the task of examining Percy's wounds, or of making any effort to restore him to consciousness.

" Good God !" he continually thought, " suppose I had married her, and this had afterwards come to light !"

And as he regarded his miserable cousin, and as he thought of all the evil which he had done, and which he seemed destined still to do, all pity for his present condition was swallowed up in loathing, and he almost prayed that it might be a corpse which lay there before him, and he felt that if——

But it was the very current of these danger-ous thoughts which brought Hammond to himself, and hastily sending his landlady for another medical man who might assist him, he set about his professional duties.

This help soon came, and they were not long in discovering the extent of the injuries which had been done.

Percy was not killed, but his state was an imminently critical one. Several bones were broken, and he had received some terrible flesh wounds; still they could not discover that he had suffered any injury which was in itself vital, and as the doctor, who had been called in, said to Hammond :

" I do not see why care and good nursing should not ultimately bring him round, but no one could answer for it. His emaciated, and evidently reduced, condition will be greatly against him, but still the tenderest care may do what nothing else can."

" And he will have it," thought Hammond to himself. " Somehow these worthless wretches always contrive to get it. Yes, he will be nursed, and cared for, and wept over, and brought back to life to be a curse to us all. Would to God he were dead, and that I could reconcile my conscience to saying nothing of his reappearance !"

But this was wild thought, and the bones having been set, and the wounds properly dressed, Hammond had immediately to decide what it behoved him to do, and what course of action he should take.

What effect would this have upon Gertrude? Of course she must be told—but how?—and would she decline to see or have anything to do with the man who had so wronged her, or, behaving after the inconsistency characteristic of her sex, take the prodigal to her bosom, and treat him as though he had never done her harm ? Would his family at Keriden receive or do anything for him, or would he become a useless burden on those who could hardly afford to help themselves ?

All these were questions which rapidly suggested themselves to Hammond, but to none of which could he find an answer ; any more than he could, at that moment, have told you whether he was sorry or glad that his marriage with Gertrude was now an impossibility; and it was with a feeling that all things were wrong, and incapable of being ever set right, that he finally determined to go and consult Minnie Tryan, on whose sound advice he felt he could best rely.

But herein he was, on this occasion, doomed to disappointment. He found Minnie at home, and alone, and so far all was well, and without much preamble he told her of what had occurred, and how Percy Rockcliffe lay at his rooms. To his intense astonishment however, Minnie, who at a crisis more than at any other time was usually to be relied upon, directly she heard and realised the fact that Gertrude's husband still lived, gave a wild hysterical laugh, and fell sobbing on the sofa, and while he stood watching her in stupefied amazement, Gertrude came in.

" Why, what is the matter?" she asked, alarmed at this unusual spectacle.

Making a sudden determination to risk all consequences, and to come straight to the point, Hammond said :

" Gertrude, I have made an unexpected and

extraordinary discovery—your husband still lives."

Gertrude's colour came and went as rapidly as the short quick breaths which she drew.

" Still lives !" she repeated in a bewildered way. " Still lives ! I hardly understand you."

In as few words as possible, Hammond told her of what had occurred, of Percy's accident, of his present dangerous condition, and of his whereabouts.

At the outset Gertrude had been grievously agitated, and to prevent herself from falling, had leant upon a chair; but as Hammond finished, she drew herself up, and said in a firmer tone than that in which she usually spoke :

" Please take me to him at once."

Here was a mystery. Minnie, whom Hammond had felt sure would give him sound, sensible advice, as to what he had best do in this extraordinary and delicate matter, was displaying inordinate weakness and emotion ; and Gertrude, whom he had dreaded to tell, and whom the affair so much more nearly affected, was bearing it with comparative calmness

" You wish me," he said, hesitating, "you wish me to take you to him ?"

" Oh, of course I do," said Gertrude, earnestly, and with the pent-up and suppressed tears starting to her eyes. " Dear Hammond, you must not let this grieve you. It must be God's will, and somehow He seems to have given me strength to bear it, and has shown me where my duty lies. Do you know I hardly feel surprised? Something has always seemed to tell me that my husband was not dead ; and though I continually banished the thought as an absurd one, in spite of myself it recurred. Now I am told that my presentiment was true. My husband is alive, but is wounded and suffering. What should I do but go to him and nurse him ? Hammond, dear friend, best of friends take me to him !"

She took his hand in hers and kissed him, as she might have kissed her brother ; and what could he do but feel that she was right, and prepare to take her with him ?

" You will come, too, Minnie ?" asked Gertrude.

Minnie, who was now herself again, and

who seemed to be somewhat ashamed of her
recent demonstration, gave a quiet consent,
and so the three set out together for Hammond's lodgings.

Arrived there Gertrude went straight into
the room in which her husband lay, while
Hammond and Minnie waited in his little
sitting-room. She was for a long time absent
from them, and it is probable that it was by
Percy's bedside that she gave way to that
emotion which hitherto she had appeared to
have been able to have almost miraculously
suppressed ; for when, after more than an hour
had elapsed, she rejoined them, though she
was quite calm and collected, and in her
demeanour was, indeed, unusually firm, the
traces in her face of the violent agitation
which she had undergone were very
evident. Minnie rose and looked at her
inquiringly.

"He is quite conscious," said Gertrude,
"and though I do not think he at all knows
where he is, he has recognised me ; and, oh,
the poor fellow did seem so pleased to see me
near him !"

It was impossible for Hammond to resist

at these words a feeling of impatience, and he said somewhat harshly :

" If you wish him to recover you must be careful not to agitate him."

" I had thought of that too," said Gertrude quietly ; " but it was necessary that I should come to him, and much, much better that he should know that his wife is with him ; but, dear Hammond, I quite agree with you, we must not expose him to the shock of any more surprises, and as you have told us that he has not hitherto recognised you, and as for many reasons the sight of you would be very painful to him, I think, if you do not mind, you had better keep away from him."

" Oh, by all means," said Hammond ironi - cally. " I do not mind in the least, and it is right that he should in every way be con- sidered. But you must remember you will want a doctor."

" Of course we shall," answered Gertrude, wholly unconscious of the irony with which he spoke ; " we must have for him the very best doctor in Blackhampton. At such a critical time as this we cannot, and must not, think of the expense. Will you, Hammond, send to me the very best doctor you know ?"

" I will do anything you wish," said Hammond, but saying it as though under compulsion.

" You are so kind and good, and I am going to ask you to do many things. I must of course stay with poor Percy, that day and night I may nurse him, and I am going to ask Minnie to stay too, and give me a little help. You will, will you not, Minnie ?"

" Of course I will !" was Minnie's hearty rejoinder.

Gertrude gave her a grateful look, and then continued :

" This seems my only plan, Hammond ; so shall you, like the good friend that you are, mind giving up your rooms to us for a time ?"

" Certainly I will," said Hammond grimly, and not trusting himself to say more.

" Thank you ! thank you a thousand times !" said Gertrude. " Now I will go to my husband again, and remain with him until you send the doctor to us."

And with this she left them. Hammond immediately took up his hat.

" Where are you going ?" asked Minnie.

" Oh !" he said quite fiercely, " I am going, in the first place, to a good doctor, to tell him I have been fortunate enough to find a case so desperate that I am incompetent to under-take it, but that I shall, all the same, have the pleasure of handing him his fees for attending to it; I shall then go and tell the landlady of my new lodgings that I shall not now require them, and haggle with her as to the amount which I must pay her for com-pensation ; then I shall go to the public-house round the corner and engage myself a bed-room for a few weeks, or a few months, or for just as long as it will take our interesting patient to recover, and until such time as his sensitive nerves will sustain the shock of being brought into contact with me. Oh, my hands are very full, I can assure you !"

Hammond was really quite ferocious, for he felt that for him the whole world was being turned upside down, and that he was the only one in it who seemed never to be con-sidered, and his temper was not improved by seeing Minnie, who was blessed with such an unfortunate sense of humour that at times it was entirely incontrollable, deliberately laugh in his face.

"Upon my word," he said, "this is too bad! You see me pushed from pillar to post, set on one side for that worthless fellow who has been the curse of my life, slighted and inconvenienced in every way, and you laugh at me!"

"I am very sorry," said Minnie, in a contrite voice, but still unable to suppress her amusement; "I am very sorry, but it does seem such a shame."

"And you find that droll? Well, I am glad that in serving others I am able to give you a certain amount of pleasure also!"

And in great indignation Hammond took his departure.

"Oh, Mr. Rockcliffe!—Hammond!" cried Minnie. "Pray come back; I did not mean to——"

But it was too late. Hammond had gone. Minnie had ceased to smile now, and indeed was sorry that she had allowed herself to do so.

But this notwithstanding, her heart, for some reason best known to herself, felt lighter than it had done for a long time.

CHAPTER VI.

RECONCILIATIONS.

CAREFULLY nursed and tended, and watched
and cared for by night and by day, Percy
began slowly to mend, and though it appeared
likely that the severe nature of his injuries
would prevent him from ever regaining his
former health and activity, it was soon manifest that they were not to prove fatal.

No one would have given Gertrude credit
for the courage, strength, and patience which
she now evinced. Her best friends had
always considered her as a feeble, and perhaps rather insufficient, little woman ; but she
now proved herself to be the most untiring,
and the firmest, as well as the kindest of
nurses. The only matters, indeed, about which
she at this time displayed anything approach-

ing to weakness, were the many proofs which she gave that she still loved tenderly her recreant, erring husband, and her extravagance as regards money.

In this last respect she seemed suddenly to have become reckless. Notwithstanding the fact that she knew that she had no money whatever of her own, and that her immediate friends could ill spare what belonged to them, she made the most unscrupulous demands upon Hammond, and with very little compunction made inroads on poor Minnie's little store, which was very soon placed at her disposal.

For herself, she would neither have done the one nor the other ; but this was not for herself. Percy lay there in mortal agony and in danger of his life. The doctor recommended for him tempting but expensive delicacies, and Gertrude felt certain that unless he had them, or that if he who had always been used to luxuries, was in his critical condition forced to live upon coarse -fare, he would certainly die. This, then, was not a time in which to indulge in false pride, or to hesitate to encroach upon her friends.

Percy's comfort and Percy's life were surely
of more importance than Minnie's and Hammond's hardly-earned pounds, and even if she
had seen the latter sitting down with a somewhat rueful face, as he now often did, to a
dinner of bread and cheese, so that the money
for Percy's oysters (at a fabulously high price),
and other dainties might be forthcoming, it is
possible that she would not very much have
cared.

Once, and once only, he endeavoured to
remonstrate with her on the question, and
then, for the first time in her life, she thought
him cruel and unkind. For his disappointment (his second disappointment) she could
feel, and though she could not but rejoice on
her own account that the man to whom she
had once and for ever given her heart had
been restored to her, she was very full of love,
tenderness, and pity for him ; but that he
should show his chagrin in hinting, rather
than saying, hard things about poor Percy ;
that he should grudge little delicacies to that
suffering martyr, this was unmanly to a
degree !

"I assure you, Gertrude," he said, "that

many of these things which you insist on buying for him are unnecessary, and it cannot last."

" They are *not* unnecessary. The doctor told me this morning that unless I induced him to take proper nourishment——"

" But flowers are not nourishment, and money is really too scarce for you to indulge every day in expensive flowers."

" You forget," said Gertrude indignantly, " that Percy has always been used to tasteful surroundings, and it is my duty to make this place as attractive as I can for him."

" But if you cannot afford it ?"

" I shall afford it as long as I can, and then, if necessary, I shall go and sing in the streets to get money for him !"

" That is absurd ; and I ought to tell you that you will not be able to afford it much longer. God knows, you are welcome to all I have, but my funds are far from being inexhaustible. You must get over your prejudice, and write to Keriden at once."

" And they will take him from me !"

" Indeed, I do not think they will do anything of the kind. My belief is that they will altogether cast him away from them. But they may render some assistance, and you ought to try them."

" And if they refuse ?"

" Then he had better go into a hospital."

Gertrude gave him a look of scorn and indignation which would have done credit to a tragedy queen, and, for his pains on her behalf, Hammond had the satisfaction of being conscious that she considered him a heartless monster.

Certainly the times were using this young man badly, and so he felt as he abruptly left the room, and nearly upset the small bearer of a savoury smelling and smoking sweetbread which was being brought in for Percy's delectation.

But his words had so far impressed Gertrude that, putting her own feelings on one side, she sat down and wrote to Keriden, telling Percy's relatives of his reappearance and present deplorable condition. It was not likely that the task would be to her a congenial one; in the time of her great trouble, and when she had been at a loss where to look for help, her husband's family had heart-

lessly ignored her, and it deeply wounded her
to write now with a confession that she required from them help, added to which she
had a great fear that they would be reconciled
to Percy, but, as the indirect cause of his
iniquities and misfortunes, would decline to
have anything to do with her ; and so foolish
was this young wife that, notwithstanding all
that had passed, she still so tenderly loved
her unexpectedly restored and erring husband,
that she looked with unspeakable dread on
anything which rendered possible a further
separation from him.

But it was necessary that before her feelings
his bodily comforts should receive attention,
and so she wrote her letter.

And Hammond wrote also, relating as
briefly as might be the facts of the case, and
telling pretty plainly of the urgent need of
help in which Percy stood ; and he too waited
somewhat anxiously for the result of the com-
munication.

They need not have agitated themselves.
To Gertrude's letter there came no answer at
all, but in reply to Hammond's, old Mr.
Rockcliffe sent an unusually voluminous

epistle, in which, however, he spoke more of his own wrongs than of his son's, and evinced a more decided desire not to commit himself than an ardent wish to receive the prodigal. A great deal was said of the " grey hairs " of which he was the proprietor being brought with " sorrow to the grave," and of the anguish which he had undergone on account of the blot which Percy's wickedness had left upon a time-honoured name. No doubt, he said, his misfortunes could for the most part be traced to the " unfortunate marriage which his son had contracted," and bearing that in mind, though he should not, if he applied for it, refuse to give him shelter, he must distinctly decline to receive again under his roof his son's wife ; nor could he, he said, undertake, so long as they remained together, to contribute anything to their support.

" H'm !" said Hammond when he had read this, " so much for my interference. She would rather that my suggestion of a hospital were carried out than this, for there she would be allowed, more or less, to see him. Well, it will be either that or the workhouse soon ;" and he looked very rueful as he drew from his pocket and chinked together a very slender stock of sovereigns, indulging the while in some rather strong language concerning his restored cousin.

But, as has been shown, Hammond was at this time frequently out of humour, and probably took a too gloomy view of things.

Slowly, but apparently surely, Percy now began to recover, and by degrees some of the details of the life which he had led since he had so hastily and cruelly deserted his wife were elicited from him. Provided, on his own confession, with a sufficient supply of ready money, he had, when he had realised the fact of how soon he would have to meet ruin face to face, betaken himself to New York, with a vague notion that in that city his wits might be turned to good account, and that he would in some way or another be able to live there after much the same fashion as that in which he had lived in England. As a matter of course, however, he had had to learn his mistake, and his money being spent, he had found himself, for the first time, left to shift on his own resources.

His first step when he found himself in

this position was not a very manly or independent one. He had written home to his father at Keriden, imploring his assistance, and, pending his reply, had lived as much as he could on credit, and, that failing, on the realisation of his personal effects, so that when he received an answer, he was already in dire necessity.

The answer was short but decisive. It came, not in the form of a parental letter, but in that of a legal epistle, written in clerkly hand, and signed by the family lawyer—a document which had evidently been subjected to the copying-press, and which very clearly and concisely stated that, after what had passed, his father felt that he could do nothing for him.

Of that which occurred after this, Percy was always reticent, though it afterwards transpired that he continued frequently to write to Keriden, representing himself to be in a state of illness and want, but never receiving any answer to his appeals. Indeed, it was no doubt best that a veil should be drawn over this period of his existence, and that, as there was one human being who still clung to him, and for the memory of bygone days still tenderly loved him, it was well that she should be spared a revelation of the straits into which this poor creature was by his self-helplessness driven.

Perhaps he told her more than he told others, but if so she kept his counsel well; and all that was ever known was that, feeling his applications to his family were useless, and rapidly falling in his own estimation and in the social scale, he was soon reduced to beggary, and then, either not feeling the inclination, or not possessing the capacity, to devote himself to any work of an elevating nature, he had himself caused the report of his death to come to England, and under an assumed name had, for a livelihood, employed himself in various ways, his last calling having been that of a groom in a circus.

His life, however, had now become a misery to him, and having been successful in winning some money on a wager, he resolved at all hazards to return to England—impelled (so he always said) by an irresistible inclination to see once more his wife. This statement, oft repeated, was a never ending source of comfort to poor Gertrude, and though Hammond received it with derision, and chose to be exceedingly unpleasant and sarcastic over it, it is perhaps charitable to give the unfortunate man the benefit of the doubt, and say that it was so.

Certainly Gertrude never heard the question doubted, for in her presence Hammond had the good taste to keep silent concerning his own views; but with others he was not equally reticent.

"But how," said Minnie, "if he did not want to see his wife, do you account for the fact that he came direct to Blackhampton, and ·to you? for he had ascertained your address, and was coming to you when the accident happened; and he had already committed his wife to your care."

"He wasn't coming to see her," said Hammond. "He was coming to try and borrow money."

"I don't think so," was the reply, "and, indeed, if you come to think of it, there was a certain amount of courage in the step which he took; for he knew that if you chose you could at once accuse him with forging Mr.

Northover's name. Now is there not something in that ?"

" A great deal," observed Hammond. " He knew very well that I was just the sort of man to take legal proceedings, and if, as you say, you ' come to think of it,' he is a perfect hero !"

But all this was, no doubt, due to spleen.

That the present state of things could long continue was of course impossible.   Work as he would, and be as liberal with his money as he undoubtedly was, it was out of the question that Hammond, who except that which he earned was possessed of nothing, could continue to support Gertrude and her husband, more especially as in the days of his illness the latter proved himself to be such a costly patient.

Ungrudgingly for Gertrude's sake, and out of contrition for his carelessness in permitting her to be defrauded of her money, he handed over every penny which he possessed, and which day by day he earned ; but the supply was wholly inadequate to the demand, and in a very short time debt had been incurred, and the poor young doctor was beset by a sea of troubles.

But just at the time when things were at their worst, and when it had become manifest that some decisive step must be taken, unexpected relief came, and it came in the person of Anthony Northover.

Since the day when Hammond had gone to his house, Gertrude had heard nothing of her uncle, and feeling herself to be deserted by him and by his family, had never once thought of seeking in that quarter for assistance ; but Anthony had a kind heart, and though he was too much influenced by others to render his niece any open or direct relief, had by no means ceased to think of her ; and from time to time, and as often as he dared, he had sent to her little presents of game and so forth, through the agency of the Triptrees, and always on the understanding that these gifts should come ostensibly from them.

But in more ways than one Anthony now began to change. Ever since he had come to Blackhampton he had done well, and receiving from his business a very good income, he had been able to live the easy life of a well-to-do middle-class tradesman, or in other words, a life after his own heart. His son-in-law and

partner—Mr. Weskut—was the active man
in their prosperous and increasing business,
and though it was not large enough to lead
to absolute affluence, there was sufficient
made out of it to keep them in very comfortable fashion, or, as Anthony put it, to enable
them to " laugh and grow fat."

Suddenly, however, the nature of this
happy-go-lucky gentleman seemed to undergo
a change. He, so to speak, " brisked up,"
and instead of being careless and indolent,
became smart, precise, and business-like, and,
what was still stranger in him, reticent ; and
he went about with an air of importance
which, among his friends and acquaintances,
gave rise to many surmises.

Now among these it was the constant
theme of conversation that Anthony was
foolish in living, as he undoubtedly did, " up
to his income," and it was, therefore, with no
little astonishment that they noted the fact
that when, on the failure of Mr. Triptree,
" Triptree's Mill" was sold by public auction,
he was the purchaser of the entire property ;
and when, soon afterwards, he removed the
jewellery business to another quarter, and

well-nigh razing that ancient structure began to erect on its site a handsome manufactory, and to lay down therein machinery of an elaborate nature, their surprise was redoubled, and it was whispered among them that he was going in for a "big thing," in which, by some person or persons unknown, he was being "backed." And it was now that he came to the assistance of his niece.

She was one day sitting and thinking anxiously of the present and of the future, when he paid her his first visit.

"My dear," he said, holding out to her both his hands, "will you shake hands with your uncle, and forgive him for having seemed to neglect you?"

Taken by surprise, and hardly knowing what to do, Gertrude gave him, without speaking, her hand, and he seemed to be wonderfully relieved.

"That's right—that's right," he said; "forget and forgive is a motto we ought all to act up to, and I'm only sorry that you should have anything to forgive me for. You must have thought me very unkind, Gertrude?"

"I did think I was unkindly treated," said she.

"My dear, it was brutish—brutish is the only word that expresses what it was, and I see it now it is too late. It would be mean now, wouldn't it, to put it all on to the women of the family—especially as your aunt and cousins mean calling here this afternoon. Will you forgive all that's past, Gertrude, and only remember it when you see how much we'll try and do for you in the future?"

"Oh, yes," said Gertrude, with a smile, "if there is anything to be forgiven. I had no very great claim upon you, and you could hardly have been expected to know of the very great trouble which I was in."

"Couldn't I?" said Anthony dubiously. "Well, never mind that now : the question is, what can I do to help you? How is your husband?"

"He is better—much better, and will, I hope, soon be strong again."

"And—you needn't mind telling me, my dear—what does he mean to do—to remain here, or to return to London?"

"I hardly know," said Gertrude, warming under the kindness of her uncle's tone, and rather glad to have the relief of talking to some one. " We are very, very badly off, and Percy says that as soon as he can he must get something to do, and he will either stay here or go elsewhere, just as anything may offer itself."

" Just so—just so," said Anthony. " Now what does he propose to look out for ?"

" He doesn't think that he could be anything but a clerk."

" With regard to his own friends," asked Anthony, " won't they do anything ?"

Gertrude shook her head.

" They are very unkind," she said, "and will do nothing—or, at least, nothing that he can think of for a moment."

" H'm," said Anthony, "as unkind as I have been. Don't be too hard on them, my dear; they may live to be as sorry for it as I am. Well, if he doesn't mind the ' come down ' of being a clerk——"

" Oh, uncle, he will not mind that. Trouble has taught poor Percy a great many lessons, and if he can only find honourable work which will support us, he will have no false pride in undertaking it."

"Very well," said Anthony, "if that is the case I think that I can help him. I'm a prosperous man, my dear, and, thank Heaven, am able to help others a little. Perhaps you've heard I'm just launching out in a new business—at least, it isn't altogether my own, because I've got a partner in it—and I'm just about engaging folks to manage it; and if your husband would like to think of it, and would really work, I think I might offer him a goodish thing. A short time ago, my dear, I took in another young fellow who had had his troubles—just as we all have 'em in our turn—and he's doing wonderful well with us, and making himself invaluable. You know young Gerald Triptree, I think? Well, that's the man. Shall I have a talk to your husband about it?"

And Anthony did have a talk with Percy, and had much difficulty in recognising in the pale, emaciated, and diffident convalescent, the supercilious young gentleman whom he had previously known; but as he very soon convinced himself that Gertrude had been right when she had said that her husband was really anxious to work, he was not very long in making him an offer, which was most gratefully accepted.

And the offer was such a liberal one that it made Percy of good heart, and did more than anything else would have done to restore to him his health and spirits.

For it seemed to tell him that there was yet left for him in the world a place in which he might be of use, and in which he might have the opportunity of redeeming some of the errors of his earlier days.

And it was with a very strong determination to do his utmost that he, for the first time, ascended a high stool in the office of the handsome building which had been erected on the site of Triptree's mill, and over the portals of which the words

"NORTHOVER AND CO.,
"PATENTEES AND MANUFACTURERS,"

were inscribed.

CHAPTER VII.

THE COMPLIMENTS OF THE SEASON.

IT was early in the new year when Percy first commenced his duties in the offices of North-over and Co., but by the time that he had earned his summer holiday he had proved, not only the earnestness of his desire to lead a steady and useful life, but also that he had it in him to become a good man of business.

Very great, indeed, was the change in his life when compared with the old days, and altogether changed was he in his habits and demeanour. He still lived with his wife in lodgings, but they were already beginning to talk of the possibility of taking for themselves a small house, and, as far as she was concerned, she contemplated with much greater satisfaction the very modest tenements which, in the course of their evening walks, they from time to time inspected, than she would have done the chance of a return to the more ostentatious establishment in Wimpole Street.

And Percy certainly deserved some amount of credit for the courage with which he discarded all his old pursuits and customs, and for the apparent contentment with which he now lived as frugally as his wife had, in Gibson Square, been used to do. To her the change was naturally satisfactory, for she felt that she was enjoying more of her husband's love and confidence than at one time she had thought to be possible, and, as compared with this, the luxury which had at one time been hers, went for nothing.

Indeed, there were only two things which at this time militated against Gertrude's complete happiness. The first of these was her sorrow for her father, of whom she could only think as of one dead, and the second her regret that Percy, notwithstanding his contentment, should set on one side, as he did, all thought of pleasure and enjoyment. To her he was now invariably loving, kind, and tender ; but it was manifest that he scrupulously avoided the society of others, holding himself aloof from all, and evidently regarding himself as one who had a ban upon him.

Percy was, without doubt, suffering from remorse; but he was doing his best to remedy the past by steadily and honestly applying himself to his work, and his wife could only hope that he would in time regain his self-respect and happiness.

Changed also was the life which the Trip-tree family were leading; but for Gerald the change was very much for the better, for not only had the troubles and disappointments which he had undergone developed all the good qualities of her whom he so dearly loved, and blessed him with a thoughtful and affectionate wife, but he had, by great good fortune, met with employment exactly to his taste, and which for himself and others he was able to turn to profitable account.

Indeed, in Northover and Co.'s new manufactory, Gerald's mechanical skill was found to be eminently useful, and a very few months sufficed to put him in so good a position in that prosperous concern, that he was able to take a modest establishment on his own account, and in it to find shelter for his father and mother.

Minnie, meanwhile, continued to work cheerfully at her old occupation, and Hammond Rockcliffe, while daily adding to his reputation and the number of his patients, kept himself in his private life exclusively to himself, and seemed likely to become a misanthrope.

Such was the state of things when the year was drawing to an end, and one and all these young people received an invitation to dine on the Christmas Day with Anthony Northover.

" Shall we go, dear ?" asked Gerald Triptree, of his wife.

" Oh, that will be just as you decide. My only regret in going would be that we should have to leave your father and mother."

" And baby ?"

" And baby, of course ; but he, dear little soul, is too young to understand, and so if you think it would be a matter of policy for us to go——"

" I would rather not put it on those grounds, Kate. Anthony Northover has been extremely kind to us, and I think we ought not to hesitate to accept his invitation."

"Then we will certainly go," said Kate; "and your views, Gerald, are quite right."

For this was the way in which, in these altered days, this young couple met each other.

While they were yet speaking of their invitation, Minnie came to them, and was immediately told of it.

"Oh, but I know all about it," said Minnie, "because I am asked too. I hope you mean to go, because I should like to, and you can take me. There is one great inducement for us. Who do you think is to be there?"

"I do not know. The Rockcliffes, possibly?"

"I do not know anything about the Rockcliffes," said Minnie, with a slight blush. "No; the mysterious partner concerning whom we have had so many conjectures, is to be there!"

"Well, it certainly will be something to meet him; and if we had not already decided to go, that would settle the matter."

"Shall we go, dear?" was the identical

question which, when they had read the somewhat ostentatious letter of invitation, written
in Mrs. Anthony's not too neat handwriting,
on gorgeous note-paper, Gertrude put to her
husband.

Percy looked somewhat troubled.

"I am not surprised to receive the invitation," he said ; " Hammond told me last night
that he had been asked, and is going. You
know, dear, what I would like to do best."

"To stay at home ?"

"Indeed I should. Alone with you."

"But I am sure that you would find them
very kind, Percy, and I know that it is their
extreme good-nature which prompts them to
ask us."

"Oh it is not that, it is not that," said
Percy. "God knows that I acknowledge
their goodness to me and value their warm-
hearted friendship. But you know, my wife,
why I never care to go where I am likely to
meet any one."

"Then for two reasons," said Gertrude
warmly, "I think you ought to go. In the
first place you must overcome that wrong
and foolish feeling ; and in the second, owing,

as we do, a great deal to my uncle's kindness, we ought not to run the risk of offending him by refusing."

And so, when Christmas morning came, the two found themselves walking together towards Anthony Northover's hospitable home. It was a bright, frosty, morning, and the soothing influence of the season stole into Gertrude's spirit, and made her full of quiet thankfulness.

"Dear Percy," she said, drawing herself closely to her husband's side, "can you help thinking to-day of the first Christmas Day which we passed together? I believe that it was the day upon which I first confessed to myself that I loved you."

Percy did not answer, and after a few moments she was surprised and distressed, on looking up at him, to see that there were tears in his eyes.

"Oh, Percy," she said, "do not grieve. Do not on this day above all others have any sad thoughts. Let us think and talk only of pleasant things to-day."

"Then we must neither think or talk of the past," he said remorsefully.

" Oh do not say that," she answered. " In their past all people have pleasant as well as sad things to recall. We have many pleasant things to remember, and it is the memory of the sad ones which makes me so grateful for our present peaceful life."

" Yes," said Percy ; " but with you it is different to what it is with me. You have been sinned against. I was always sinning! I can never think of the past without reproaching myself."

" But not in everything," said Gertrude. " Surely there are some things which you may think of with satisfaction ?"   ·

" I believe there are none, or at all events it seems to me that whenever an episode of the past is recalled it brings with it the recollection of some injury which I have done. For example, you speak of the first Christmas Day which we spent together, and immediately there comes before me the scene in which, respecting that very day and his hospitality to me, I most cruelly insulted your father. You may imagine, Gertrude, the extent to which I feel my treatment of him when I tell you that with the memory of all my shortcomings and wickedness before me, with the anticipation of the well-merited reproaches which he would heap upon me, I should be thankful to meet him face to face and assure him of my desire to do better in the future."

"Poor papa !" said Gertrude with tears in her eyes, " I wonder, Percy, whether we shall ever again hear of him ? Every one tells me that he must be dead, but to me that seems to be impossible, and I do not know whether it is more dreadful to think of him so or of his living so far away without one word of love from me !"

Their conversation was at this point interrupted by their meeting with Gerald Triptree and his wife, who, coming along a side-road, suddenly appeared. Being bound for the same place the two young couples naturally joined company, and the talk assumed a more cheerful tone. Gerald was in high spirits, and soon made Gertrude laugh by a description of the scene which he had left behind him in his own home, where his father and mother (who had declined Anthony Northover's invitation) were occupied in minding the baby and preparing their own Christmas dinner.

At their host's comfortable house they now very soon arrived, and found that preparations for spending Christmas on a sumptuous scale and with the most suitable surroundings had been made. The house had been made a very bower of evergreens, and gorgeously illuminated Christmas legends and mottoes, studded with red holly and white mistletoe-berries, decorated the walls in every direction.

Anthony Northover, too, was in what he himself called " great form," and greeting his guests in a most exuberant manner, ushered them into the portly presence of Mrs. North-over, who, dressed in the richest brown satin, awaited them in her many-coloured drawing-room.

Here, too, flushed with excitement, were all the young Northovers, including "young Fred," who was talking quietly in a corner to a rosy-cheeked, blue-eyed, and flaxen-haired young lady attired in pink silk and white kid boots, and who had lately been introduced to his family as his betrothed ; on the hearthrug stood Mr. Weskut, who apparently had retained all his old taste for resplendent jewellery, and who was giving to Hammond Rockcliffe, who had already arrived, his opinions as to the state of the nation, albeit Hammond, though respectfully attentive, found it difficult to fix his eyes upon this orator, and found them continually wandering to another part of the room, where Minnie Tryan was surrounded by a small crowd of the most juvenile members of the party admiring their multifarious Christmas presents.

Handsome presents had indeed been the order of the day, and, teeming with generosity, the warm-hearted Anthony had found it impossible to resist making a small offering to each of his visitors, and so Minnie had been already presented with a pretty pair of ear-rings, Hammond with a set of shirt-studs, and Gerald and Kate had not been in the house ten minutes before they were the delighted possessors of (just the very thing Kate had wanted!) a substantial perambulator.

"You see I've made it a double one in case of accidents, my dear," said Anthony in an

undertone to Kate, and at the same time
" nudging " Gerald ; and then without waiting to see the effect of this piece of pleasantry,
he bustled off to Gertrude.

" And now, my dear, you must come and
see what I've got for you. It's in another
room, and your husband's not to see it until
I know whether you like it or not."

Gertrude laughed lightly, and immediately
left the room with him, not however before
Anthony had exchanged with his wife a look
full of meaning.

They were away for a time, which, to
those who were left, seemed to be inordinately
long, and the conversation lagged as before-
dinner conversations always do lag, even
among the most genially-disposed people.
Even Mr. Weskut's flow of oratory ceased,
and he relapsed into commonplace observa-
tions about the seasonableness of the weather ;
Hammond unsuccessfully endeavoured to sustain a conversation with Mrs. Northover,
Minnie had to rack her brain for materials
wherewith to amuse the food-expectant little
people, while " young Fred " and his flaxen-
haired *fiancée* began to wish for an inter-

ruption to their prolonged *tête-à-tête*; and all were thinking to themselves that the delay in the appointed hour for dinner betokened a want of management on the part of their host and hostess, which was not only exceedingly inauspicious, but was all the more provoking because of its being so unexpected.

At length, however, Anthony reappeared, but not to bring with him the much longed for announcement that "dinner was on the table," but merely to beckon mysteriously to Percy and to disappear with him.

This was too much. All of the guests had appreciated the generosity of their host, and had been pleasantly surprised at the presents which they had received, but this was carrying things rather too far. If the giving of Gertrude's present was to occupy so much time, it certainly should have been delayed until after dinner. And so they relapsed into a prolonged and almost sullen silence until——

Until the door again opened, and with on one side of him Gertrude, with a supremely happy but withal greatly agitated face, and on the other Percy, and supported also by

Anthony, who was so smiling through tears
that it seemed almost natural to look for a
rainbow on the opposite wall, Godfrey Northover entered the room.

Hammond was so close to this apparition
that he had no time to obey his first impulse,
and rush from the room and from the presence of the man whom he so much dreaded
to meet, and before his amazement would
allow him to stir he found himself most
warmly shake hands with and greeted as an
old and dear friend.

The thing was well managed. In a moment
dinner was announced, Hammond was re-
quested to offer his arm to Mrs. Northover,
and in a few moments he found himself seated
between that lady and Godfrey Northover,
whom Anthony had introduced to the rest of
the company as his " senior partner."

And Godfrey Northover talked to Hammond as though nothing which could possibly
estrange them had happened. Without
making any formal statement, and with far
greater tact than Hammond had ever thought
him capable of displaying, he let him, between
the courses of thick soup, boiled cod-fish, roast

beef, turkey, plum-pudding, and cheese, with which the party were regaled, understand as follows :

Ever since he had left England he had been in America—principally in New York. His health had been restored to him, and with it his old aptitude and desire for business, and he had in many small speculations, more for the sake of killing time than of gaining money, carefully embarked. His silence had been part of a set plan. He had believed that Gertrude was in all ways well provided for, and that her chances of happiness would be increased by his absence, and, deeply as he felt the estrangement from her, he determined for her sake to endure it. So things had gone on with him, and if he had led an unhappy, he had at least lived a busy life. About the time of Percy's reappearance in England, however, he had met with, and become the proprietor of, several most valuable patents, which he felt sure could in his own country be worked to the greatest advantage ; and thinking to benefit his brother Anthony, he had communicated with him, and for the first time since his emigration had allowed his English friends to know that he was in the land of the living. From Anthony he had speedily learned the whole truth concerning Gertrude and her husband, and, enjoining upon him the strictest secrecy, he had formed a plan, which he hoped now to bring to a happy conclusion. The chief features of this plan were that he and his brother were to become partners in the manufacturing and selling of the various patents, of which mention has been already made; that Percy should be offered a situation with the new firm, and that if he showed a real desire to work, and to redeem the past, and to become a good husband, a partnership should be offered to him; furthermore, Anthony was enjoined to report progress to his brother, and when every item of this plan was in good working order, Godfrey was to show himself.

On this Christmas Day that happy period had arrived, and being anxious that the past should be forgotten, he avowed himself to be a happy man.

He was certainly a more convivial and a more communicative man than Hammond had ever yet known him to be, and when, the cloth being withdrawn, the table groaned beneath the weight of the decanters of wine, the dishes of nuts, of French plums, of oranges, of apples, of almonds and raisins, of preserved fruits and ginger, of cakes and fancy biscuits, of figs, hot chestnuts, and foreign grapes, which constituted Mrs. Northover's idea of a Christmas Day dessert—he could hardly believe that it was the Godfrey North-over, who, in days gone by, had lived in Gibson-square, Islington, who rose and call-ing attention to himself seemed anxious to make a speech.

"Anthony," he said, "may I ask of you what is the correct wine in which to drink a toast of importance ?"

Here there was much applause and several differently expressed opinions. Mr. Weskut declared loudly in favour of "port," "young Fred" was for "Madeira," others were for sherry, and one or two of the ladies spoke of claret.

"I believe," resumed Godfrey, "that I am right in saying that on special occasions a sparkling wine commonly, I fancy, termed "champagne" is drunk. This is a very special occasion, and if I am right in my surmise, and my brother, who seems to have in his house everything that is seasonable and good, happens to have that peculiar wine in his cellar, I would call for 'champagne.'"

The credit of Anthony's cellar was at stake, and the wine was at once ordered, notwithstanding the fact that Mr. Weskut whispered rather loudly to Percy, who happened to be his near neighbour, that "fizz after dinner was out of all form, you know."

Luckily for his guests, Anthony's champagne was of an excellent brand, and, when the wine sparkled and creamed in the crystal glasses, there was not a single malcontent at the table.

Feeling that he had done the correct thing, Godfrey rose again.

"I merely desire," he said, "to wish one and all here a 'Merry Christmas.' Never until to-day did I realise the fact that Christmas could be merry, and therefore I wish it you with the greater heart. In speaking of Christmas I naturally revert to the new year,

and in the new year I think of our new business.   In that business we have 'young
blood' (here he nodded to Percy and gave
also a kindly glance at Gerald), and with
energy we are sure to meet with success. My
friends and my daughter, this is, notwithstanding sad reminiscences, which a man at
my time of life cannot expect to be without,
the happiest Christmas of my life, and I
trust that none of you will experience a less
happy one."

He sat down amid rapturous applause, and
the loudly, but heartily, expressed good wishes
which were on all sides now exchanged, and
the merry clinking together of the wine
glasses, were pleasant to hear.

Every one at the table seemed to have a
light heart and a happy face.   Every one ?
No.   Hammond Rockcliffe, strive as he would
and did, felt that he could neither look happy
in face nor feel light at heart, and so when,
very soon after Godfrey's speech was over,
the formal sitting at the dinner table was, in
favour of a general circle round the fireside,
broken up, he, making an excuse, left the
room to try and reason with himself, and if

possible to make some show of feeling the same enjoyment which manifestly pervaded the rest of the company.

But somehow he felt that he could not do so. Standing alone in the deserted drawing-room and gazing through the window at the fast declining day, bitter thoughts arose within him, and he felt that while some who deserved nothing seemed to have all things, he, who had at least made it one of his aims in life to help others, lacked all things, and was alone in the world. For his happiness there was something wanted——

Almost noiselessly the door opened, and it was not until he felt himself lightly touched that he became suddenly aware that that "something" stood by his side.

" I have come to take you back," said Minnie; "they are already inquiring for you."

"I do not think that I shall go back," he said. " My black face will only act as a cloud upon the rest."

"But it is only black in your imagination," she replied. "Do you think that none of us there have our troubles to bear ?"

" Of course, of course," he said, " but mine sometimes seems too hard to bear."

They were silent for a few moments, and though the room was growing so dark that she could scarcely see him, Minnie knew that he was striving hard to keep back his tears.

" Why should you bear your trouble any longer ?" she said in a very low tone.

" Minnie !" he cried with a new tone of energy in his voice, and a new light in his face : " Do you mean it—do you realise what my trouble is ?"

" Am I your trouble ?" she asked.

" Oh, Minnie ! you know it !"

" Then let your trouble be always near you."

And in a moment she was very near him. It was a moment that decided the happiness of their lives.

The room was quite dark and the stars were out when he said to her :

" But why, Minnie, did you so often and so steadfastly refuse me ?"

" Because, Hammond, I had told myself, and I believed most firmly, that I should best ensure the happiness of your life by doing so."

" And now, dearest ?"

" I begin to believe—and oh how good it is to believe it !—that you love me so dearly and so truly, that without me happiness would never be yours."

And soon after that they rejoined the Christmas fire-side circle, and among those who formed it there was not a single heavy heart.

THE END.

Works by the same Author.

UNDER PRESSURE. A Novel. In Two Volumes.

OPINIONS OF THE PRESS.

" So little of what is pleasant falls to the lot of the Reviewer, that he may be pardoned for dwelling on the compensations of his galling trade. Shenstone, in his ' Essays on Men and Manners,' remarks that critics remind him of 'certain animals called asses, which by nibbling vines taught men the advantage of pruning them.' Without presuming to continue this metaphor, a humble critic may urge another plea in self-defence. The critic's rod of hazel is as often a divining twig as an instrument of correction, and merit, that lies like hidden waters beneath the surface, is often first brought to light by the prescience of the expert. Thus much the critic may plead in excuse for his existence, which, to the thinking of the authors, needs very frequent excuse. The preamble is suggested by ' Under Pressure,' by T. E. Pemberton, a novel which, though by certain weak and wavering touches betraying the inexperienced hand, is yet a novel above the average standard, and full of promise for the future. . . . . We will not detail the dramatic end of this interesting and well-written story."—*Daily News, March 4th,* 1875.

" 'Under Pressure' is the title of a very pleasant two volume novel by Mr. T. E. Pemberton. . . . . There is humour, character, and much clever description in ' Under Pressure,' and it is sure to be read with interest."—*Yorkshire Post, December 24th,* 1874.

" The plot is uncommonly well arranged, and the interest is well maintained, from the first page to the last. . . . . Mr. Pemberton has given us a very good, very readable, very attractive story of ordinary life, with just a dash or two of sensation ; and having thoroughly appreciated his labours, we can strongly recommend his two volumes to the novel-reading world."—*Birmingham Daily Post, March 24th,* 1875.

"The book has very considerable vigour and originality. The character of the hero, Hugh Haslip, is drawn with no little force and truth."—*Scotsman, January 26th,* 1875.

" Unlike most of the novels of the present day, it (' Under Pressure ') is not a story full of the most dramatic and sensational occurrences and situations ; it is something better —a homely story—a story of real life. . . . Mr. Pemberton's descriptive powers are decidedly great, and will doubtless, as he gains experience, increase. He has a good appreciation of character, and the whole of his character sketches are well drawn."—*Birmingham Daily Gazette, January 19th*, 1875.

" It (' Under Pressure ') is possessed of considerable merit, and the plot is interesting and well sustained. . . . . It is a thoroughly sound, honest, sensible story ; it teaches nothing but what is good, and does not contain a line of sickly sentimentalism, nor any unhealthy sensationalism."—*Midland Counties Herald, March 18th*, 1875.

" Mr. Pemberton has proved himself an interesting story-teller, and we are pleased to recommend his ' Under Pressure' to both young and old."—*Liverpool Town Crier, January 9th*, 1875.

" In reading ' Under Pressure,' we see that the author has minutely studied character. . . . . His appreciation of goodness, his sorrow for evil, and his contempt for what is mean, are truly admirable. Suffice it to say, that Mr. Pemberton has displayed keen observation, and high literary capacity."—*Birmingham Morning News, January 22nd*, 1875.

CHARLES LYSAGHT. A Novel devoid of
Novelty. In Two Volumes.

OPINIONS OF THE PRESS.

" An honest attempt to pourtray character, and to depict scenes of actual life as they have fallen under the author's own observation. The hero and his father are both well delineated, and the struggles of the former, in his effort to gain a living by his own exertions, are described in a painfully vivid manner, but without any undue colouring."—*Daily News, March 5th*, 1874.

" The story grows very painful as it pictures the hopeless struggle of the boy-husband and his bright, loving, girl-wife. The author touches his work with a firm distinctness at this point exceedingly realistic and powerful."—*Literary World, April 10th*, 1874.

" There are some sketches of character and many descriptive passages by no means wanting in skill."—*Era, December 28th*, 1873.

" Notwithstanding the title, there is a 'novelty' about this novel which will be found very refreshing."—*Alfreton Journal, December 5th*, 1873.

" There are some scenes and sentiments of considerable merit."—*Tablet, December 13th*, 1873.

" Two or three of the minor portraits are uniques. . . . We beg to commend the novel in general. . . . . No circulating library ought to be without it."—*Illustrated Review, December 27th*, 1873.

" Natural gifts do not seem wanting, and there is a power displayed both of perception and characterisation."—*Sunday Times, January 4th*, 1874.

" In ' Charles Lysaght ' we have a novel which is thoroughly enjoyable, from the first page of vol. i. to the last of vol. ii."—*Court Express, January 10th*, 1874.

" There is a great interest and not a little dramatic power all through the book. . . . Most of the characters are graphically sketched, and well individualised, but the chief charm is the continuous interest of the narrative, and the skill with which the tale is told."—*Birmingham Daily Post, April 4th*, 1874.

" It is written in an easy, pleasant style."—*Bookseller, January*, 1874.

DICKENS'S LONDON; OR, LONDON IN THE WORKS OF CHARLES DICKENS.

By T. EDGAR PEMBERTON,

AUTHOR OF " UNDER PRESSURE," ETC., ETC.

Price 6s., post free, and of all Booksellers.

OPINIONS OF THE PRESS.

" Mr. Pemberton has ' invented ' a very new style of book, and has carried out his idea with excellent industry and marked success. . . . All admirers of the works of Charles Dickens will thank Mr. Pemberton for a very original and very interesting book."—*Birmingham Daily Post, December 17th*, 1875.

"So happily conceived, that we are surprised no one thought of producing such a work before. . . . Mr. Pemberton's book is well worth reading."—*Newcastle Weekly Chronicle, January 29th,* 1876.

"Mr. T. Edgar Pemberton is to be thanked and congratulated for having industriously collected into a single volume most of the passages about the 'little village' which occur in the several novels of the inimitable Dickens."—*Christmas Bookseller,* 1875—76.

"There are passages in the book which show that Mr. Pemberton possesses humour and considerable power of description on his own account."—*Yorkshire Post, January 6th,* 1876.

"Mr. Pemberton presents a panorama of London, delineated by Dickens' own graphic pencil, which cannot fail to attract."—*Northampton Mercury, January 29th,* 1876.

"It is therefore to lovers of the works of Dickens, not resident in London, that the book will be of the greatest interest, whether they intend to make their next visit to London an opportunity of performing a pilgrimage to some of the shrines indicated in his writings, or whether they will be content, as 'stay-at-home travellers,' to make the imagination do duty for the actual investigation ; in either case the perusal of the volume now under notice will not fail to be appreciated either as a guide for the one or the gratification of the other."—*Brighton Examiner, January 29th,* 1876.

"Mr. Pemberton has, in the most attractive and compact form, culled from the works of Dickens the various scenes depicted by the great author in most of his works, as having occurred in London. . . . . and his own remarks, with which the work is largely taken up, bear the impress of being written by a true admirer of a great author."—*Wiltshire County Mirror, February 1st,* 1876.

"Any lover of Charles Dickens (and who is not ?) will be interested to have recalled to his mind the various places described by the author."—*Bath and Cheltenham Gazette, February 2nd,* 1876.

"Mr. Pemberton's conception was a happy one. . . . . Many will thank Mr. Pemberton for identifying and mapping out localities associated with what Dickens has written."—*Carlisle Patriot, February 4th,* 1876.

"The writer has visited in person all the scenes of which he makes mention; and where Dickens' description was necessarily limited, he has explained and added, and that too, in such a lucid manner as has, combined with his easy style and evident knowledge of his subject, rendered his book eminently readable. . . . . We would recommend his book to all readers of Charles Dickens."—*Bradford Observer*, *February 5th*, 1876.

" Mr. Pemberton's descriptions of the London localities named in ' Pickwick,' ' Oliver Twist,' ' Nicholas Nickleby,' ' Barnaby Rudge,' etc., give fresh interest to the works themselves, and form an appropriate and welcome supplement to them. No admirer of Dickens should be without this book."—*Hastings and St. Leonards News, February 4th*, 1876.

" We turn to the index at the end of the volume, and discover that the list of places referred to falls little short of three hundred in number. Mr. Pemberton has rightly judged that the public, and especially the London public, would be glad to have these references brought together, and to know a little more of the places which the great inventor has peopled with his creations."—*Hereford Times Literary Miscellany, February 5th*, 1876.

" It would, perhaps, be claiming too much for this book to say that without it the writings of Dickens would be incomplete, but without doubt it furnishes a very valuable supplement to them. . . . It is a book full of interest, and one that we can recommend without reservation."—*Sunderland and Durham County Herald, February 11th*, 1876.

" Mr. Pemberton's idea is an excellent one, and it is pleasantly and profitably worked out in this single volume. . . To all lovers of Dickens this book will be specially welcome. An index of places facilitates reference, and makes the volume additionally interesting and useful."—*Public Opinion, March 4th*, 1876.

" A sensibly arranged index renders the volume handy for reference, and greatly adds to its practical utility."—*Richmond and Twickenham Times, March 11th*, 1876.

" In numerous cases the writer has taken such care in hunting up doubtful localities and identifying somewhat dubious descriptions as evidences a commendable striving after accuracy, and a by no means slight knowledge of his subject." —*East Anglian Daily Times, February 28th*, 1876.

" Such a book could not fail to be of interest, and it must be said that Mr. Pemberton has skilfully executed the task he has imposed upon himself. . . . We certainly welcome Mr. Pemberton's book, and can strongly recommend it to the admirers of the great writer of whose works it treats."—*Kendal Mercury, February 12th*, 1876.

" A very readable and instructive book."—*Wakefield Express, February 5th,* 1876.

" Much ingenuity is displayed in the identification of the various localities, and the book will be a serviceable guide to any who may be disposed to trace out such localities for themselves."—*Hampshire Advertiser, February 5th,* 1876.

" We have here a work of great interest and merit. . . . The work is one which we can cordially recommend to all who delight in reading Dickens."—*Poole and South Western Herald, February 10th,* 1876.

" Mr. Pemberton has taken from the several stories the localities and scenes of most stirring interest, and has woven them into a pleasant, gossipy series of chapters. . . . It will be found full of interest as a companion volume to Dickens's works."—*Leeds Mercury, February 9th,* 1876.

" Mr. Pemberton has already made several very successful ventures in literature, and the present one will not detract from his reputation for careful and industrious workmanship. . . . The author has visited every nook or highway in London to which Dickens anywhere alluded. . . . . The book is one to call up pleasant memories, and all the more so because its compiler has done his work so well."—*Oxford and Cambridge Undergraduates' Journal, February 3rd,* 1876.

" The book will be acceptable to the public, as adding to their knowledge of the words of the great novelist."—*Halifax Times, February 8th,* 1876.

" The writer frankly admits that the part which he plays in this book is ' simply comparable to a showman of a panorama of London, whereof Dickens was the painter,' and the reader of his book must as frankly admit that a very enjoyable ' showman ' he has proved himself to be."—*Gloucester Mercury, February 12th,* 1876.

" Those who are fond of odd books will have quite a prize in the one we have placed at the head of this notice. ' Dickens's London ' is really both a curious as well as a readable book, and is worthy a place in every library."—*Rochdale Observer, February 5th,* 1876.

" The volume is beautifully got up, and the information is to the readers of Dickens's works of a specially interesting kind, and we believe that before long it will find a place on the shelves of every well selected library."—*Barnsley Chronicle, February 5th,* 1876.

"It is to indulge this feeling—to enable others to share with him the peculiar pleasure of identifying with the original a house, a court, a lane, or a street described by Dickens, that Mr. Pemberton has undertaken his task. . . . . We can testify to the pleasure with which we have perused his book."
—*Reading Mercury, February 12th,* 1876.

"The author has carefully compiled the delineations of London life with which Dickens' incomparable novels abound, and they are cleverly worked up into this handsomely bound volume."—*Shrewsbury Chronicle, February 18th,* 1876.

"The sketches are neatly strung together, and Mr. Pemberton's comments are pointed. Altogether the book is one of the most concise, chatty, and readable ones which have been published about London, and as such we commend it to lovers of Dickens, and people interested in the first city of the world."
—*Liberal Review, February* 19th, 1876.

"The work is very interesting, and is evidently the result of careful and painstaking labour."—*Preston Herald, February 19th,* 1876.

"A valuable volume, and one which no one would regret reading."—*Banbury Advertiser, February 10th,* 1876.

"Mr. Pemberton's selections have been made with great skill and judgment."—*Huddersfield Daily Chronicle, February 23rd,* 1876.

"The several chapters furnish a variety of reading of a light and gossiping description, conveying in connection with the text of passages in Dickens' immortal works, topographical and anecdotical information, which will no doubt be acceptable in many quarters."—*Bristol Mercury, February 26th,* 1876.

"It would be impossible to do otherwise than compliment Mr. Pemberton on the manner in which he has written his book."—*Nottingham Daily Guardian, March 3rd,* 1876.

LONDON : SAMUEL TINSLEY, 10, SOUTHAMPTON STREET, STRAND, W.C.

SAMUEL TINSLEY'S

PUBLICATIONS.

𝔏onɗon :

SAMUEL TINSLEY,

10, SOUTHAMPTON STREET, STRAND.

⁎ *Totally distinct from any other firm of Publishers.*

60

NOTICE.

MR. SAMUEL TINSLEY begs to intimate that he is now prepared to undertake the PRINTING and PUBLICATION of ALL CLASSES OF BOOKS, Pamphlets, &c.—Apply to MR. SAMUEL TINSLEY, Publisher, 10, Southampton Street, Strand, London, W.C.

*** ALL COMMUNICATIONS AND MANUSCRIPTS SHOULD BE DISTINCTLY ADDRESSED AS ABOVE, AND WILL RECEIVE PROMPT ATTENTION.

A SACRIFICE TO HONOUR. By Mrs. HENRY
LYTTELTON ROGERS. Crown 8vo, 7s. 6d.

AS THE FATES WOULD HAVE IT. By G.
BERESFORD FITZGERALD. Crown 8vo., 10s. 6d.

A WOMAN TO BE WON. An Anglo-Indian
Sketch. By ATHENE BRAMA. 2 vols., 21s.
"She is a woman, therefore may be wooed ;
She is a woman, therefore may be won."
—TITUS ANDRONICUS, Act ii., Sc. 1.
"A welcome addition to the literature connected with the most picturesque of our dependencies."—*Athenæum*.
"As a tale of adventure "A Woman to be Won" is entitled to decided commendation."—*Graphic*.
"A more familiar sketch of station life in India . . . . has never been ritten. . . . ."—*Nonconformist*.

BARBARA'S WARNING. By the Author of " Recommended to Mercy." 3 vols., 31s. 6d.

BETWEEN TWO LOVES. By ROBERT J. GRIFFITHS, LL.D. 3 vols., 31s. 6d.

BLUEBELL. By Mrs. G. C. HUDDLESTON. 3 vols.,
31s. 6d.
"Sparkling, well-written, spirited, and may be read with certainty of amusement."—*Sunday Times*.

BORN TO BE A LADY. By KATHERINE HENDERSON. Crown 8vo, 7s. 6d.

BRANDON TOWER. A Story. 3 vols., 31s. 6d.
"Familiar matter of to-day."

BREAD UPON THE WATERS: a Novel. By MARIE
J. HYDE. Crown 8vo, 7s. 6d.

BUILDING UPON SAND. By ELIZABETH J.
LYSAGHT. Crown 8vo., 10s. 6d.
"We can safely recommend 'Building upon Sand.'"—*Graphic*.

CHASTE AS ICE, PURE AS SNOW. By Mrs.
M. C. DESPARD. 3 vols., 31s. 6d. Second Edition.
"A novel of something more than ordinary promise."—*Graphic*.

CINDERELLA: a New Version of an Old Story.
Crown 8vo, 7s. 6d.

CLAUDE HAMBRO. By JOHN C. WESTWOOD. 3
vols., 31s. 6d.

COOMB DESERT. By G. W. Fitz. Crown 8vo., 7s. 6d.

CORALIA; a Plaint of Futurity. By the Author of "Pyrna." Crown 8vo, 7s. 6d.

CRUEL CONSTANCY. By Katharine King, Author of 'The Queen of the Regiment.' 3 vols., 31s. 6d.

DISINTERRED. From the Boke of a Monk of Carden Abbey. By T. Esmonde. Crown 8vo., 7s. 6d.

DR. MIDDLETON'S DAUGHTER. By the Author of "A Desperate Character." 3 vols., 31s. 6d.

DULCIE. By Lois Ludlow. 3 vols., 31s. 6d.

EMERGING FROM THE CHRYSALIS. By J. F. Nicholls. Crown 8vo, 7s. 6d.

FAIR, BUT NOT FALSE. By Evelyn Campbell. 3 vols., 31s. 6d.

FAIR, BUT NOT WISE. By Mrs. Forrest-Grant. 2 vols., 21s.

FAIR IN THE FEARLESS OLD FASHION. By Charles Farmlet. 2 vols., 21s.

FIRST AND LAST. By F. Vernon-White. 2 vols., 21s.

FLORENCE; or, Loyal Quand Même. By Frances Armstrong. Crown 8vo., 5s., cloth. Post free.

"A very charming love story, eminently pure and lady-like in tone."—*Civil Service Review.*

FOLLATON PRIORY. 2 vols., 21s.

FOR TWO YEARS. By Vectis. Crown 8vo., 7s. 6d.

FRANK AMOR. By Jajadee. 3 vols., 31s. 6d.

FRIEDEMANN BACH; or, The Fortunes of an Idealist. Adapted from the German of A. E. Brachvogel. By the Rev. J. Walker, B.C.L. Dedicated, with permission, to H.R.H. the Princess Christian of Schleswig-Holstein. 1 vol., crown 8vo, 7s. 6d.

GAUNT ABBEY. By Elizabeth J. Lysaght, Author of "Building upon Sand," "Nearer and Dearer," etc. 3 vols., 31s. 6d.

GERALD BOYNE. By T. W. EAMES. 3 vols., 31s. 6d.

GILMORY. By PHŒBE ALLEN. 3 vols., 31s. 6d.

GOLD DUST. A Story. 3 vols., 31s. 6d.

GOLDEN MEMORIES. By EFFIE LEIGH. 2 vols., 21s.

GRAYWORTH: a Story of Country Life. By CAREY HAZELWOOD. 3 vols., 31s. 6d.

GRANTHAM SECRETS. By PHŒBE M. FEILDEN. 3 vols. 31s. 6d.

GREED'S LABOUR LOST. By the Author of "Recommended to Mercy," etc. 3 vols., 31s. 6d.

HER GOOD NAME. By J. FORTREY BOUVERIE. 3 vols., 31s. 6d.

HER IDOL. By MAXWELL HOOD. 3 vols., 31s. 6d.

HILDA AND I. By MRS. WINCHCOMBE HARTLEY. 2 vols., 21s.

"An interesting, well-written, and natural story."—*Public Opinion*.

HILLESDEN ON THE MOORS. By ROSA MAC-KENZIE KETTLE, Author of "The Mistress of Langdale Hall." 2 vols., 21s.

HIS LITTLE COUSIN. By EMMA MARIA PEARSON, Author of "One Love in a Life." 3 vols., 31s. 6d.

IN BONDS, BUT FETTERLESS: a Tale of Old Ulster. By RICHARD CUNINGHAME. 2 vols., 21s.

IN SECRET PLACES. By ROBERT J. GRIFFITHS, LL.D. 3 vols., 31s. 6d.

IN SPITE OF FORTUNE. By MAURICE GAY. 3 vols., 31s. 6d.

INTRICATE PATHS. By C. L. J. S. Cr. 8vo., 7s. 6d.

IS IT FOR EVER? By KATE MAINWARING. 3 vols., 31s. 6d.

JABEZ EBSLEIGH, M.P. By Mrs. EILOART, author of "The Curate's Discipline," "Meg," "Kate Randal's Bargain," etc. 3 vols., 31s. 6d.

JOHN FENN'S WIFE. By MARIA LEWIS. Crown 8vo., 7s. 6d.

KATE BYRNE. By S. HOWARD TAYLOR. 2 vols. 21s.

KATE RANDAL'S BARGAIN. By Mrs. EILOART, Author of "The Curate's Discipline," "Some of Our Girls," "Meg," &c. 3 vols., 31s. 6d.

KITTY'S RIVAL. By SYDNEY MOSTYN, Author of 'The Surgeon's Secret,' etc. 3 vols., 31s. 6d.

LADY LOUISE. By KATHLEEN ISABELLE CLARGES. 3 vols., 31s. 6d.

LALAGE. By AUGUSTA CHAMBERS. Crown 8vo, 7s. 6d.

LASCARE : a Tale. 3 vols., 31s. 6d.

LEAVES FROM AN OLD PORTFOLIO. By ELIZA MARY BARRON. Crown 8vo, 7s. 6d.

LIFE OUT OF DEATH: a Romance. 3 vols. 31s. 6d.

LLANTHONY COCKLEWIG: an Autobiographical Sketch of His Life and Adventures. By the Rev. STEPHEN SHEPHERD MAGUTH, LL.B., Cantab. 3 vols., 31s. 6d.

LORD CASTLETON'S WARD. By Mrs. B. R. GREEN. 3 vols., 31s. 6d.

LOVE THE LEVELLER : a Tale. Crown 8vo., 7s. 6d.

MADAME. By FRANK LEE BENEDICT, Author of "St. Simon's Niece," etc. 3 vols., 31s. 6d.

MARGARET MORTIMER'S SECOND HUSBAND. By Mrs. HILLS. 1 vol., 7s. 6d.

MARJORY'S FAITH. By FLORENCE HARDING. Crown 8vo, 7s. 6d.

MART AND MANSION : a Tale of Struggle and Rest. By PHILIP MASSINGER. 3 vols., 31s. 6d.

MARTIN LAWS: a Story. Crown 8vo, 7s. 6d.

MARRIED FOR MONEY. 1 vol., 10s. 6d.

MARY GRAINGER: A Story. By George Leigh.
2 vols., 21s.

MAUD LEATHWAITE: an Autobiography. By
Beatrice A. Jourdan, Author of "The Journal of
a Waiting Gentlewoman." Crown 8vo., 7s. 6d.

MR. VAUGHAN'S HEIR. By Frank Lee Benedict,
Author of " Miss Dorothy's Charge," etc. 3 vols., 31s. 6d.

MUSICAL TALES, PHANTASMS, AND
SKETCHES. From the German of Elise Polko.
By M. Prime Maudslay. Dedicated (with permission) to Sir
Julius Benedict. Crown 8vo, 7s. 6d.

NEARER AND DEARER. By Elizabeth J.
Lysaght, Author of "Building upon Sand." 3 vols.,
31s. 6d.

NEGLECTED; a Story of Nursery Education Forty
Years Ago. By Miss Julia Luard. Crown 8vo., 5s.
cloth.

NO FATHERLAND. By Madame Von Oppen.
2 vols., 21s.

NORTONDALE CASTLE. 1 vol., 7s. 6d.

NOT TO BE BROKEN. By W. A. Chandler.
Crown 8vo., 10s. 6d.

ONE FOR ANOTHER. By Emma C. Wait.
Crown 8vo, 7s. 6d.

ONLY SEA AND SKY. By Elizabeth Hindley.
2 vols., 21s.

OVER THE FURZE. By Rosa M. Kettle, Author
of the " Mistress of Langdale Hall," etc. 3 vols., 31s. 6d.

PENELOPE'S WEB: a Story. By Louis Withred.
3 vols., 31s. d.

PERCY LOCKHART. By F. W. Baxter. 2 vols.,
21s.

PUTTYPUT'S PROTÉGÉE; or, Road, Rail, and
River. A Story in Three Books. By HENRY GEORGE
CHURCHILL. Crown 8vo., (uniform with "The Mistress of
Langdale Hall"), with 14 illustrations by WALLIS MACKAY.
Post free, 4s. Second edition.

"It is a lengthened and diversified farce, full of screaming fun and
comic delineation—a reflection of Dickens, Mrs. Malaprop, and Mr.
Boucicault, and dealing with various descriptions of social life. We have
read and laughed, pooh-poohed, and read again, ashamed of our interest,
but our interest has been too strong for our shame. Readers may do
worse than surrender themselves to its melo-dramatic enjoyment. From
title-page to colophon, only Dominie Sampson's epithet can describe it—it
is 'prodigious.'"—*British Quarterly Review.*

RAVENSDALE. By ROBERT THYNNE, Author of
"Tom Delany." 3 vols., 31s. 6d.

REAL AND UNREAL: Tales of Both Kinds. By
HARRIET OLIVIA BODDINGTON. Crown 8vo., 7s. 6d.

ROSIE AND HUGH; or, Lost and Found. By HELEN
C. NASH. 1 vol., crown 8vo., 6s.

RUPERT REDMOND: A Tale of England, Ireland,
and America. By WALTER SIMS SOUTHWELL. 3 vols.,
31s. 6d.

ST. NICOLAS' EVE, and other Tales. By MARY C.
ROWSELL. Crown 8vo., 7s. 6d.

SAINT SIMON'S NIECE. By FRANK LEE BENEDICT,
Author of "Miss Dorothy's Charge." 3 vols., 31s. 6d.

From the **Spectator**, July 24th:—"A new and powerful novelist has arisen
. . . We rejoice to recognise a new novelist of real genius, who knows and
depicts powerfully some of the most striking and overmastering passions of
the human heart . . . It is seldom that we rise from the perusal of a story
with the sense of excitement which Mr. Benedict has produced."

SELF-UNITED. By Mrs. HICKES BRYANT. 3 vols.,
31s. 6d.

SHE REIGNS ALONE: a Novel. By BEATRICE
YORKE. 3 vols. 31s. 6d.

SHINGLEBOROUGH SOCIETY. 3 vols., 31s. 6d.

SIR MARMADUKE LORTON. By the Hon. A. S. G.
CANNING. 3 vols., 31s. 6d.

SKYWARD AND EARTHWARD: a Tale. By
ARTHUR PENRICE. 1 vol., crown 8vo, 7s. 6d.

SOME OF OUR GIRLS. By Mrs. EILOART, Author of "The Curate's Discipline," "The Love that Lived," "Meg," etc., etc. 3 vols., 31s. 6d.

"A book that should be read."—*Athenæum.*

SO SINKS THE DAY STAR: The Story of Two Lovings and a Liking. By JAMES KEITH. Crown 8vo., 7s. 6d.

SONS OF DIVES. 2 vols., 21s.

SPOILT LIVES. By MRS. RAPER. Crown 8vo, 7s. 6d.

SQUIRE HARRINGTON'S SECRET. By GEORGE W. GARRETT. 2 vols., 21s.

STANLEY MEREDITH : a Tale. By "SABINA." Crown 8vo, 7s. 6d.

STILL UNSURE. By C. VANE, Author of "Sweet Bells Jangled." Crown 8vo, 7s. 6d.

STRANDED, BUT NOT LOST. By DOROTHY BROMYARD. 3 vols., 31s. 6d.

SWEET IDOLATRY. By MISS ANSTRUTHER. Crown 8vo, 7s. 6d.

THE ADVENTURES OF MICK CALLIGHIN, M.P. a Story of Home Rule ; and THE DE BURGHOS, a Romance. By W. R. ANCKETILL. In one Volume, with Illustrations. Crown 8vo, 7s. 6d.

THE BARONET'S CROSS. By MARY MEEKE, Author of "Marion's Path through Shadow to Sunshine." 2 vols., 21s.

THE BRITISH SUBALTERN. By an Ex-SUBALTERN. 1 vol., 7s. 6d.

THE CLEWBEND. By MOY ELLA. Crown 8vo., 7s. 6d.

THE CRIMSON STAR. By J. EDWARD MUDDOCH. 3 vols., 31s. 6d.

THE D'EYNCOURTS OF FAIRLEIGH. By THOMAS ROWLAND SKEMP. 3 vols., 31s. 6d.

THE DAYS OF HIS VANITY. By SYDNEY GRUNDY. 3 vols., 31s. 6d.

THE HEIR OF REDDESMONT. 3 vols., 31s. 6d.

THE INSIDIOUS THIEF: a Tale for Humble Folks. By One of Themselves. Crown 8vo., 5s. Second Edition.

THE LOVE THAT LIVED. By Mrs. EILOART, Author of " The Curate's Discipline," "Just a Woman," " Woman's Wrong," &c. 3 vols., 31s. 6d.

" Three volumes which most people will prefer not to leave till they have read the last page of the third volume."—*Pall Mall Gazette.*

" One of the most thoroughly wholesome novels we have read for some time." —*Scotsman.*

THE MAGIC OF LOVE. By Mrs. FORREST-GRANT, Author of " Fair, but not Wise." 3 vols., 31s. 6d.

" A very amusing novel."—*Scotsman.*

THE MASTER OF RIVERSWOOD. By Mrs. ARTHUR LEWIS. 3 vols., 31s. 6d.

THE MISTRESS OF LANGDALE HALL: a Romance of the West Riding. By ROSA MACKENZIE KETTLE. Complete in one handsome volume, with Frontispiece and Vignette by PERCIVAL SKELTON. 4s., post free.

" The story is interesting and very pleasantly written, and for the sake of both author and publisher we cordially wish it the reception it deserves." —*Saturday Review.*

THE RING OF PEARLS; or, His at Last. By JERROLD QUICK. 2 vols., 21s.

THE SECRET OF TWO HOUSES. By FANNY FISHER. 2 vols., 21s.

THE SEDGEBOROUGH WORLD. By A. FARE-BROTHER. 2 vols., 21s.

THE SHADOW OF ERKSDALE. By BOURTON MARSHALL. 3 vols, 31s. 6d.

THE STAR OF HOPE, and other Tales. By VICTORIA STEWART. Crown 8vo, 7s. 6d.

THE SURGEON'S SECRET. By SYDNEY MOSTYN, Author of " Kitty's Rival," etc. Crown 8vo., 10s. 6d.

" A most exciting novel—the best on our list. It may be fairly recommended as a very extraordinary book."—*John Bull.*

Samuel Tinsley, 10, Southampton Street, Strand.

THE THORNTONS OF THORNBURY. By Mrs.
HENRY LOWTHER CHERMSIDE. 3 vols., 31s. 6d.

THE TRUE STORY OF HUGH NOBLE'S
FLIGHT. By the Authoress of "What Her Face Said."
10s. 6d.

THE WIDOW UNMASKED; or, the Firebrand in
the Family. By FLORA F. WYLDE. 3 vols., 31s. 6d.

THE WOMAN THAT SHALL BE PRAISED. A
Story. Crown 8vo., 7s. 6d.

THE YOUTH OF THE PERIOD. By J. F. SHAW
KENNEDY, Esq., late 79th Highlanders. Cr. 8vo., 7s. 6d.

TIMOTHY CRIPPLE; or, "Life's a Feast." By
THOMAS AURIOL ROBINSON. 2 vols., 21s.

TIM'S CHARGE. By AMY CAMPBELL. 1 vol., crown
8vo, 7s. 6d.

TOO FAIR TO GO FREE. By HENRY KAY WIL-
LOUGHBY. 3 vols., 31s. 6d.

TOO LIGHTLY BROKEN. 3 vols., 31s. 6d.

"A very pleasing story . . . . . very prettily told."—*Morning Post.*

TOM DELANY. By ROBERT THYNNE, Author of
"Ravensdale." 3 vols., 31s. 6d.

"A very bright, healthy, simply-told story."—*Standard.*
"There is not a dull page in the book."—*Scotsman.*

TOWER HALLOWDEANE. 2 vols., 21s.

TOXIE: a Tale. 3 vols., 31s. 6d.

'TWIXT CUP and LIP. By MARY LOVETT-CAMERON.
3 vols., 31s. 6d.

'TWIXT HAMMER AND ANVIL. By FRANK LEE
BENEDICT, Author of "St. Simon's Niece," "Miss Dorothy's Charge," etc. 3 vols., 31s. 6d.

'TWIXT WIFE AND FATHERLAND. 2 vols.,
21s.

"It is by someone who has caught her (Baroness Tautphoeus') gift of
telling a charming story in the boldest manner, and of forcing us to take
an interest in her characters, which writers, far better from a literary point
of view, can never approach."—*Athenæum.*

TWO STRIDES OF DESTINY. By S. Brookes Bucklee. 3 vols., 31s. 6d.

UNDER PRESSURE. By T. E. Pemberton. 2 vols., 21s.

WAGES: a Story in Three Books. 3 vols., 31s. 6d.

WANDERING FIRES. By Mrs. M. C. Despard, Author of " Chaste as Ice," &c. 3 vols., 31s. 6d.

WEBS OF LOVE. (I. A Lawyer's Device. II. Sancta Simplicitas.) By G. E. H. 1 vol., Crown 8vo., 10s. 6d.

WEIMAR'S TRUST. By Mrs. Edward Christian. 3 vols., 31s. 6d.

WHAT OLD FATHER THAMES SAID. By Coutts Nelson. 3 vols., 31s. 6d.

WHO CAN TELL? By Mere Hazard. Crown 8vo., 7s. 6d.

WILL SHE BEAR IT? A Tale of the Weald. 3 vols., 31s. 6d.

"This is a clever story, easily and naturally told, and the reader's interest sustained throughout. . . . A pleasant, readable book, such as we can heartily recommend."—*Spectator*.

WOMAN'S AMBITION. By M. L. Lyons. 1 vol., 7s. 6d.

YE OUTSIDE FOOLS! or, Glimpses INSIDE the Stock Exchange. By Erasmus Pinto, Broker. A New Edition. Crown 8vo., price 5s.

Public Opinion says ;—"Written in a clever, cynical, and incisive style, and thoroughly exposes the rigs and tricks of the Stock Exchange. One advantage of a perusal will be that those who allow themselves to be plundered will do so quite consciously. The volume as a whole is extremely interesting."

YE VAMPYRES! A Legend of the National Betting Ring, showing what became of it. By the Spectre. In striking Illustrated Cover, price 2s., post free.

Samuel Tinsley, 10, Southampton Street, Strand.

ROBA D'ITALIA; or, Italian Lights and Shadows:
a record of Travel. By CHARLES W. HECKETHORN. In 2
vols., 8vo, price 30s.

THE EMPEROR AND THE GALILEAN: a Drama
in two parts. Translated from the Norwegian of HENRIK
IBSEN, by CATHERINE RAY. In 1 vol., crown 8vo, 7s. 6d.

ETYMONIA. In 1 vol., crown 8vo, 7s. 6d.

HOW I SPENT MY TWO YEARS' LEAVE; or, My
Impressions of the Mother Country, the Continent of
Europe, the United States of America, and Canada. By an
Indian Officer. In one vol., 8vo. Price 12s.

FACT AGAINST FICTION. The Habits and
Treatment of Animals Practically Considered. Hydro-
phobia and Distemper. With some remarks on Darwin. By
the HON. GRANTLEY F. BERKELEY. 2 vols., 8vo., 30s.

MALTA SIXTY YEARS AGO. With a Concise
History of the Order of St. John of Jerusalem, the
Crusades, and Knights Templars. By Col. CLAUDIUS SHAW.
Handsomely bound in cloth, 10s. 6d., gilt edges, 12s.

HARRY'S BIG BOOTS: a Fairy Tale, for "Smalle
Folke." By S. E. GAY. With 8 Full-page Illustrations
and a Vignette by the author, drawn on wood by PERCIVAL
SKELTON. Crown 8vo., handsomely bound in cloth, price 5s.

"Some capital fun will be found in ' Harry's Big Boots.'. . . The illustrations are excellent, and so is the story."—*Pall Mall Gazette.*

MOVING EARS. By the Ven. Archdeacon WEAKHEAD,
Rector of Newtown, Kent. 1 vol., crown 8vo., 5s.

THE PHYSIOLOGY OF THE SECTS. Crown
8vo., price 5s.

ANOTHER WORLD; or, Fragments from the Star
City of Montalluyah. By HERMES. Third Edition, re-
vised, with additions. Post 8vo.; price 12s.

AMONG THE CARLISTS. By JOHN FURLEY, Author
of " Struggles and Experiences of a Neutral Volunteer."
Crown 8vo., 7s. 6d.

THE DOCTRINE OF THE EVERLASTING TOR-
MENT OF THE WICKED SHOWN TO BE UN-
SCRIPTURAL. In wrapper, Price 1s.

PUZZLES FOR LEISURE HOURS. Original and
Selected. Edited by THOMAS OWEN. In ornamental
wrapper. Price 1s. (post free.)

THE REGENT : a play in Five Acts and Epilogue
J. M. CHANSON. Crown 8vo., 5s.

THE RITUALIST'S PROGRESS ; or, A Sketch of the
Reforms and Ministrations of the Rev. Septimus Alban,
Member of the E.C.U., Vicar of S. Alicia, Sloperton. By
A B WILDERED Parishioner. Fcp. 8vo. 2s. 6d. cloth.

EPITAPHIANA; or, the Curiosities of Churchyard
Literature : being a Miscellaneous Collection of Epitaph,
with an INTRODUCTION. By W. FAIRLEY. Crown 8vo., cloth.
price 5s. Post free.

" Entertaining."—*Pall Mall Gazette.*
" A capital collection."—*Court Circular.*
" A very readable volume."—*Daily Review.*
" A most interesting book."—*Leeds Mercury.*
" Interesting and amusing." *Nonconformist.*
" Particularly entertaining."—*Public Opinion.*
" A curious and entertaining volume."—*Oxford Chronicle.*
" A very interesting collection."—*Civil Service Gazette.*

POEMS AND SONNETS. By H. GREENHOUGH
SMITH, B.A. Fcap, 8vo, 3s. 6d.

GRANADA, AND OTHER POEMS. By M. SABISTON.
Fcp. 8vo., 4s.

HELEN, and other Poems. By HUBERT CURTIS.
Fcp. 8vo., 3s. 6d.

SUMMER SHADE AND WINTER SUNSHINE :
Poems. By ROSA MACKENZIE KETTLE, Author of " The
Mistress of Langdale Hall." New Edition. 2s. 6d., cloth.

CANTON AND THE BOGUE : the Narrative of an
Eventful Six Months in China. By WALTER WILLIAM
MUNDY. Crown 8vo, 7s. 6d.

DICKENS'S LONDON : or, London in the Works of
Charles Dickens. By T. EDGAR PEMBERTON, Author of
" Under Pressure." Crown 8vo, 6s.

Samuel Tinsley, 10, Southampton Street, Strand.

SYRIA AND EGYPT UNDER THE LAST FIVE SULTANS OF TURKEY ; being the Experiences during Fifty Years of Mr. Consul-General Barker, with Explanatory Remarks to the Present Day, by his son, EDWARD B. B. BARKER, H.B.M. Consul.   In 2 vols., 8vo.

A NARRATIVE OF TRAVEL AND SPORT IN BURMAH, SIAM, AND THE MALAY PENINSULA. By JOHN BRADLEY.   Post 8vo., 12s.

TO THE DESERT AND BACK ; or, Travels in Spain, the Barbary States, Italy, etc., in 1875-76. By ZOUCH H. TURTON.   One vol., large post 8vo.

ITALY REVISITED.   By A. GALLENGA (of *The Times*), Author of " Country Life in Piedmont," &c., &c. 2 vols., 8vo., price 30s.   Second Edition.

The Times says—" Mr. Gallenga's new volumes on Italy will be welcome to those who care for an unprejudiced account of the prospects and present condition of the country.   Most interesting volumes."

UNTRODDEN SPAIN, and her Black Country. Being Sketches of the Life and Character of the Spaniard of the Interior. By HUGH JAMES ROSE, M.A., of Oriel College, Oxford. In 2 vols., 8vo., price 30s. (*Second Edition.*)

The Times says—" These volumes form a very pleasing commentary on a land and a people to which Englishmen will always turn with sympathetic interest."

The Saturday Review says—" We can only recommend our readers to get it and search for themselves.   Those who are most intimately acquainted with Spain will best appreciate its varied excellences."

OVER THE BORDERS OF CHRISTENDOM AND ESLAMIAH ; or, Travels in the Summer of 1875 through Hungary, Slavonia, Bosnia, Servia, Herzegovina, Dalmatia, and Montenegro to the North of Albania. By JAMES CREAGH, Author of " A Scamper to Sebastopol." 2 vols., large post 8vo, 25s.

"May be safely recommended."—*World.*

SOCIAL ARCHITECTURE ; or, Reasons and Means for the Demolition and Reconstruction of the Social Edifice. By AN EXILE FROM FRANCE. Demy 8vo., 16s.

OUR INDIAN EMPIRE: the History of the Wonderful Rise of British Supremacy in Hindustan. By the Rev. SAMUEL NORWOOD, B.A., Head Master of the Grammar School, Whalley. Crown 8vo, 7s. 6d.

Samuel Tinsley, 10, Southampton Street, Strand.

10, SOUTHAMPTON STREET, STRAND.

June 20th, 1877.

SAMUEL TINSLEY'S
NEW PUBLICATIONS.

BOOKS OF THE DAY.

NOTICE.—Important New Work by Mr. GALLENGA.

TWO YEARS OF THE EASTERN QUES-TION.

By A. GALLENGA (of the *Times*), Author of "Italy Revisited," "Country Life in Piedmont," "The Invasion of Denmark," etc. 2 vols. 8vo., price 28s.

A NEW AND CHEAPER EDITION OF

TRAVELS WEST.

By WILLIAM MINTURN. Large post 8vo, price 7s. 6d.

"A charming book, full of anecdotes of Western American travel, and in which the author, who travelled from New York across the whole American Western desert, gives his experience of a country almost unknown to European colonists. We wish we could transcribe some of the very clear descriptions of scenery, life, and manners in which this book abounds."—*Public Opinion.*

NEW AND CHEAPER EDITION OF "YE OUTSIDE FOOLS."

YE OUTSIDE FOOLS ; or, Glimpses Inside the Stock Exchange.

By ERASMUS PINTO, Broker. Crown 8vo., 5s.

"Written in a clever, cynical, and incisive style, and thoroughly exposes the 'rigs and tricks of the Stock Exchange. One advantage of a perusal will be that those who allow themselves to be plundered will do so quite consciously. The volume as a whole is extremely interesting."—*Public Opinion.*

THERESE HENNES, AND HER MUSICAL EDUCATION : a Biographical Sketch.

By her FATHER. Translated from the German MS. by H. MANN-HEIMER. Crown 8vo, 5s.

THE RISE AND DECAY OF THE RULE OF ISLAM.

By ARCHIBALD J. DUNN. Large post 8vo, 12s.

NOTES AND ESSAYS ON THE CHRISTIAN RELIGION : Its Philosophical Principles and its Enemies.

By JOHN JOSEPH LAKE. Crown 8vo., price 7s. 6d.

DIFFICULTIES OF POLITICAL ECONOMY.

By a YOUNG BEGINNER. Crown 8vo., price 2s. 6d.

POPULAR NEW THREE-VOLUME NOVELS.

NOTICE.—New Story by the Popular Author of "The Curate's Discipline," "Woman's Wrong," "Just a Woman," etc.

HIS SECOND WIFE.

By Mrs. EILOART, Author of "Meg," "Just a Woman," "Woman's Wrong," etc.   3 vols. 31s. 6d.

NOTICE.—The Important Story of Russian Life by Prince Joseph Lubomirski.

TATIANA ; or, The Conspiracy.

A Tale of St. Petersburg.   By Prince JOSEPH LUBOMIRSKI. 3 vols. 31s. 6d.

"The story is painfully interesting."—*Standard.*

NOTICE.—The New and Popular Story by the Author of "Recommended to Mercy," "Taken upon Trust," etc.

DONE IN THE DARK.

By the Author of "Recommended to Mercy."   3 vols. 31s. 6a.

NOTICE.—The Popular New Novel by the Author of "Brown as a Berry" and "The Red House by the River."

MAR'S WHITE WITCH.

By GERTRUDE DOUGLAS, Author of "Brown as a Berry," etc. 3 vols. 31s. 6d.

"A thoroughly good novel, which we can cordially recommend to our readers. . . . We should not have grudged a little extra length to the story ; . . . . for 'Mar's White Witch' is one of those rare novels in which it is a cause of regret, rather than of satisfaction, to arrive at the end of the third volume."—*John Bull.*

AGAINST HER WILL.

By ANNIE L. WALKER, Author of "A Canadian Heroine." 3 vols. 31s. 6d.

RIDING OUT THE GALE.

By ANNETTE LYSTER.   3 vols. 31s. 6d.

"The tale is full of stirring incident, and one or two of the character creations—notably Singleton's sister Hadee—are finely conceived and artistically developed."—*Scotsman.*

JESSIE OF BOULOGNE.

By the Rev. C. GILLMOR, M.A.   3 vols. 31s. 6d.

THE RECTOR OF OXBURY: a Novel.

3 vols. 31s. 6d.

BITTER TO SWEET END: a Novel.

3 vols. 31s. 6d.

THE SEARCH FOR A HEART: a Novel.

By JOHN ALEXANDER.   3 vols. 31s. 6d.

TRUE WOMEN.

By KATHARINE STUART.   3 vols. 31s. 6d.

A VERY OLD QUESTION.
By T. EDGAR PEMBERTON, Author of "Under Pressure," "Dickens's London," etc. 3 vols. 31s. 6d.

THE SIEGE OF VIENNA: a Novel.
By CAROLINE PILCHER. (From the German.) 3 vols. 31s. 6d.

A VERY OLD QUESTION: a Novel.
By T. EDGAR PEMBERTON, Author of "Under Pressure," etc. 3 vols. 31s. 6d.

"For 'tis a question left us yet to prove,
Whether love lead fortune or else fortune love."—*Hamlet.*

POPULAR NEW NOVELS, ETC.,
Each complete in ONE VOLUME.

THE WOMAN THAT SHALL BE PRAISED: a Novel.
By HILDA REAY. I vol. crown 8vo, price 7s. 6d.

"Decidedly well written, attractive, and readable . . . . . . The characters stand out as if they had been pondered over and worked at ; the circumstances are fresh and natural ; the style is pure, and the thoughts refined."—*Athenæum.*

"Besides the heroine there is another 'woman that shall be praised,' viz., the authoress. Praised for writing in English, for some passages of poetry, for some even of slang, for her boldness and tenderness of expression, and, above all, for writing a religious novel without shocking us with pious utterances."—*Public Opinion.*

"Well written ; and the household of the thriftless doctor is described with humour and a considerable insight into character."—*Daily News.*

"The story is a pleasant one to read, and the minor characters are sketched with a good deal of discrimination and humour."—*John Bull.*

"The charm of this novel lies in the character of the heroine, the young lady to whom the title refers . . . . . . the good angel of the house."—*Court Circular.*

A NEW-FASHIONED TORY.
By "WEST SOMERSET." I vol. crown 8vo, 7s. 6d.

RENRUTH.
By HENRY TURNER. Crown 8vo, 7s. 6d.

SIBYLLE'S STORY.
By OCTAVE FEUILLET. Translated by MARGARET WATSON. Crown 8vo, 7s. 6d.

A DISCORD: a Story.
By ALETH WILLESON. I vol. crown 8vo, 7s. 6d.

"The story is gracefully and thoughtfully written, and there is a distinct impress of realism about most of the personages."—*Scotsman.*

VAGABOND CHARLIE.
By "VAGABOND." I vol. crown 8vo, 7s. 6d.

CLARA PONSONBY: a Novel.
By ROBERT BEVERIDGE. I vol. crown 8vo, 7s. 6d.

ADAM AND EVE'S COURTSHIP; or, How to Write a Novel.
By JAY WYE. Crown 8vo, price 7s. 6d.

THE BRIDE OF ROERVIG.

By W. BERGSOE. Translated from the Danish by NINA FRANCIS. Crown 8vo, 7s. 6d.

TOUCH NOT THE NETTLE : a Story.

By ALEC FEARON. Crown 8vo, 7s. 6d.

THROUGH HARDSHIPS TO LORDSHIP.

By FLORA EATON. Crown 8vo. 7s. 6d.

DAISY AND THE EARL

By CONSTANCE HOWELL. Crown 8vo, 7s. 6d.

THE VANDELEURS OF RED TOR. A Tale of South Devon.

By THEODORE RUSSELL MONRO. Crown 8vo, 7s. 6d.

THE LADY BLANCHE.

By HAROLD ST. CLAIR. Crown 8vo, 7s. 6d.

HARRINGTON : a Novel.

By FREDERICK SPENCER BIRD. Crown 8vo., price 7s. 6d.

THE BURIED PAST : a Novel.

Crown 8vo., price 7s. 6d.

LAMECH ; or, the Two Wives. A Tale.

To which is added " The Daughters ; or, Hannah and Peninnah." Crown 8vo., 3s. 6d.

"And Lamech took unto him two wives ; the name of one was Adah, and the name of the other Zillah."—GEN. iv. 19.
"Elkanah, an Ephrathite, had two wives ; the name of the one was Hannah, and the name of the other Peninnah."—1 SAM. i., 1, 2.

EXCELLENT BOOKS FOR THE YOUNG.

Now ready, in one very handsome volume, with a number of graphic Coloured Illustrations, price 5s. post free, and of all Booksellers.

THE ADVENTURES OF TOM HANSON ;

Or, Brave Endeavours Achieve Success ; a Story for Boys. By FIRTH GARSIDE, M.A.

ROSIE AND HUGH ; a Tale for Boys and Girls.

By HELEN C. NASH. 1 vol crown 8vo, 6s.

" In 'Rosie and Hugh' we have all the elements of fiction presented in the best possible form to attract boys and girls. Wholesome, pure, lively, with here and there a dash of humour, the book is certain to be a favourite with both parents and children . . . A cheerful, clever work."—Morning Post.

SEED-TIME AND REAPING. A Tale for the Young.

By HELEN PATERSON. Crown 8vo. 5s.

LONDON :

SAMUEL TINSLEY, 10, SOUTHAMPTON STREET, STRAND.

www.ingramcontent.com/pod-product-compliance
Lightning Source LLC
Chambersburg PA
CBHW020900020726
47497CB00005B/1493